The Quest

The Quest
A Tale of Desire
& Magic

HEATHER STRANG

RiverWood Books
Ashland, Oregon

RiverWood Books is an imprint of White Cloud Press.
RiverWood Books titles may be purchased for educational, business, or sales
promotional use. For information, please write: Special Market Department,
RiverWood Books, PO Box 3400, Ashland, OR 97520
Website: www.whitecloudpress.com

Cover art by Jim Thomson: http://jimkirkthomson.com/
Cover and Interior Design by C Book Services

First edition: 2014
14 15 16 17 18   10 9 8 7 6 5 4 3 2 1

Printed in the United States of America

Library of Congress Cataloging-in-Publication Data
Strang, Heather (Reiki healer)
The quest : a tale of desire & magic : / Heather Strang.
    pages cm
ISBN 978-1-940468-22-8 (pbk.)
1. Spiritual biography--Fiction. 2. Spiritual life--Fiction. I. Title.
PS3619.T739Q47 2014
813'.6--dc23
                        2014030126

For all the loves that led me here.
And to the Universe who makes every day in my life magic.
Thank you.

Acknowledgements

The book that you are holding in your hands was co-created by myself and the Universe from a state of pure positive energy, connection and magic. It has been infused with powerful healing energy that will allow you to align more fully to who-you-really-are. Enjoy and welcome the synchronicities, aha's and insights you gain while reading it. Trust that the events that occur as you are immersed in this book are of the highest divine order and are part of your continual alignment with the Source within you.

The journey of writing *The Quest* and having it now in your hands was one that continually surprised and delighted me. And it reminded me of this core truth: whatever we can imagine is only a fraction of that which the Universe can deliver. Case in point...

In April 2011 during a meditation, I was told I would write novels. I had never before written fiction and brushed off this "guidance." Then, on a May 2011 trip to St. Louis and while in the Cathedral Basilica I was given more guidance about the nature of the novel (it would be spiritual romance! WTF?!) and I was told I must return to the Cathedral during a specific year in the future (more on that surely to come). Still, I doubted this "guidance" as I was a journalist by trade and a poet—mostly in secret—unless you count the 2009 publication of *Anatomy of the Heart—Love Poems*.

Then, after seeing Esther Hicks and Abraham in June 2011 and as I was driving home from the half day event, the entire story that you see in the pages that follow downloaded into my consciousness. Just. Like. That.

I wrestled with allowing this book to come forth into the world, resisting it at every turn, certain that it was not my path to write spiritual romance novels. But, one's truth is persistent, and I was consistently guided again and again to finish the novel.

Within one month of self-publishing it in June 2012, I was approached by film director Lee Scharfstein and shortly thereafter *The Quest* was optioned as a film. A year after self-publishing it, I was approached by *White Cloud Press* to publish *The Quest, Following Bliss* and *And Then It Was You* to a larger audience and in paperback.

These experiences have taught me so much including the fact that anything is possible. And I mean anything. It requires soul alignment, it requires listening, it requires only taking inspired action and it requires trust. When all of this aligns, magic is your everyday experience.

And with that I have to thank many of the great healers and teachers in my life who have been a support to me: John of God, Abraham-Hicks, John Veltheim, Paulo Coelho, Anaiya Sophia, my various BodyTalk practitioners and mentors (Gilly Adkins, Dr. Janet Galipo, Dr. Laura Stuve, Shelley Poovey, Christine Barrie, Sid Snider), my angels and guides of the highest light and so many more!

Thank you to the team at White Cloud Press. You all just rock. I knew from our first email exchange signed "Much love" that Spirit had brought me the perfect publisher!

I am extremely grateful to everyone in my life who encouraged and believed in my ability to create outside of my comfort zone and has stayed the course with me through this magical journey. You know who you are. And I love you so.

May all of our lives be filled with magic, sumptuous desire, and bliss. It is, after all, our birthright.

Xo Heather

Chapter 1

*"Ever since time began, people have recognized their true
Love by the light in their eyes." –Paulo Coelho*

"You will spend your life with a man named Matthew," said the psychic, as the light within his dark brown eyes danced. "You two will be very much in love and will live in Europe, where he will oversee a sustainable farm. You will have two children—girls—named Stacy and Allison."

Kathryn Casey sat captivated. At 30-years-old, this was information she had been waiting to receive ever since she heard her first love story. Now, sitting before her was a man with the answer. Samorio was a South African native and had spent his entire life traveling the world, sharing the information he received from Spirit. To a person off the street, Samorio may not have appeared to hold answers to the greatest mysteries within—he was in his late-fifties, with a gleaming bald head, and wearing all white clothing. Yet, he had come highly recommended by Kathryn's girlfriend Hillary and her husband Paul, who had been relying on Samorio's guidance for years; and they were the happiest couple Kathryn knew.

Five years ago, when Hillary considered leaving the marriage (she had been with Paul since her early-twenties, and the excitement of singledom called to her), they had gone to Samorio and he had skillfully guided them back to one another. His work with them had, according to Hillary, allowed her to look at the deeper reasons for her discontent. He was even able to share some past life experiences with Hillary that brought her back to her senses.

Kathryn was engaged in one of the most important quests of her life: finding her true love. She had spent years dating and having relationships with perfectly fine men, but none of them had that staying power she longed for. She was at her wits' end and she wasn't willing to leave it to chance anymore. So, when - six months earlier - Kathryn broke down in front of Hillary and Paul about her frustration over being unable to find her soul mate, they knew it was time to call in the big guns. Getting a psychic reading from just *anyone* wasn't an option. She needed the best.

Kathryn remembered the turn of events perfectly.

They were in Hillary and Paul's spacious kitchen, as she started to cry and covered her face. They rushed to soothe her, and were incredibly kind and understanding, telling Kathryn that someday she would find The One. They each carried that sympathetic, yet pitiful, look on their faces while Hillary lightly rubbed her back and Paul rattled off a list of men he knew—categorically assessing which ones might be a good match for Kathryn. (None of them were; as much as she liked Paul, she was rather loathing of the engineering type. They bored her half to death!) However, this time something was different. Maybe it was because Kathryn had never cried about her frustration in front of them before, but this time they gave her a resource beyond just the name and number of one of Paul's coworkers.

Standing around the kitchen island with dark cherry wood and granite, glasses of Merlot in hand, Kathryn wiped the mascara from her tear-stained cheeks and ran her hands through her long brown curls, attempting to gather herself. Paul slyly looked over at Hillary, who nodded, and then he scurried over to his desk. Kathryn had thought it all a bit peculiar, but had been too busy with her self-induced angst to give it much thought. Paul, his black hair curly and unruly, adjusted his glasses, looked Kathryn in the eye and said, "Hillary and I both think it's time to call in the best for your 'Quest.'"

"Wh-what is it?" Kathryn turned to Hillary for more explanation. Hillary's blue eyes sparkled as she stood there looking at Kathryn, her dirty blonde hair pulled to one side, her hands placed lightly on her curvy hips. It was no wonder she found love so early in life—she was one of the kindest people Kathryn knew *and* she was absolutely gorgeous.

"Honey," Hillary came over and put her hand on Kathryn's back. "We think you should see Samorio."

Kathryn gasped.

"The psychic?!"

"Yes. As you know, we've used him for virtually everything in our life and he's never been wrong."

"But, do you really think he can give me substantial information about my soul mate?" Kathryn said in disbelief.

Kathryn had been to a few other intuitives over the past few years, but none of them were any help at all when it came to finding love.

"We know that a lot of psychics give false information about this type of thing," Paul said. "But, we really want to encourage you to schedule a session with him. If anyone can give you information that will lead to the great love of your life, it's this guy."

Kathryn was stunned. Had it really come to this? A psychic to help her find The One? Well, maybe it had. Stranger things had happened. She had tried eHarmony at one point, so it couldn't hurt to go see Samorio, who was reportedly never wrong about anything.

As Kathryn headed home that night, Hillary gave her a warm hug and made her promise she would text her as soon as she set up an appointment with Samorio. It was because of all of this that Kathryn felt quite safe in not only paying a strange man from South Africa to foretell her future, but also in receiving wisdom that she herself had been unable to access. It had been a dark wet night when she visited Hillary and Paul, but when she left, the clouds had dried up and in its place blew a strong wind.

She stood outside looking up at the stars and smiled. Her heart felt hopeful. Maybe she would find him after all.

The Quest for her soul mate started so long ago, it was impossible for Kathryn to pinpoint when it began. At some time during her early childhood, she had this knowing that she would spend the rest of her life with one man. That they would travel the world together, have hot sex (of course!), support one another through all of life's ups and downs, work together in some capacity (as a freelance writer, she wasn't sure how that would manifest, but she imagined she and her One would run some type of empire together), and spend their down time laughing, cooking, and meditating. While this description regularly made her girlfriends gag, it was a vision that continually plagued her. She just couldn't shake it.

Yes, it was cheesy, overplayed and over-fantasized, but no matter how hard Kathryn tried to put her focus elsewhere, it remained. In fact, other than writing, it was the only thing that had stuck with Kathryn for so long.

It was not, as one might imagine, a popular fantasy for Kathryn— or any woman in the 21st century for that matter—to hold onto. She had spent years listening to first her mother, then her sister Audrey, and countless friends throughout her 30 years, telling her that love wasn't magical—it was chemical and from there you simply made a decision about who you would spend your life with. Anything cosmic or otherworldly was out of the question. Her mother consistently warned her that falling in love was not like falling in love in a movie. Of course, this line was delivered with a pointed finger wagging in Kathryn's face. Couldn't Kathryn be like everyone else and marry someone who was practical (her mother's words, words that made Kathryn groan in pain) and who she could buy a house with, then pop out a few kids, and spend her days driving a minivan to soccer practice like all the "normal" women in the world? Couldn't Kathryn be okay with spending weekends taking trips to Costco, consuming more goods than her family needed, and eating ice cream in the evenings?

No, Kathryn could not.

In fact, the very thought of doing the "practical" thing made her feel like she was going to die. Literally, it was as if she might fall over and die whenever she imagined her life the way her mother saw it. So, while everyone in her world—including Hillary and Paul—said that love was not like a movie, some part of Kathryn knew that magical love *did* exist. At least for her. She didn't know why she believed this or how it might be different for her than other people in the world, but something inside of her told her there was more than the relationships and love she saw around her, and that she herself had experienced.

She had tried to give it all up, though—tried to believe that magical love was simply for the movies. There was that one time, after finding out her love was a closet daily marijuana smoker (how had she missed that?!) that she gave up on love. She was so disgusted with herself and the Universe that she threw her hands up in mock repulsion and said the words she never thought she would utter: "I give up! He doesn't exist. You win!" She had finally succumbed to all the negative talk from family and friends, and accepted her fate. If she wanted love, it would have to be practical love. Ick.

Immediately, she dove into her work. As a successful freelance writer, she was able to work from her cozy home office, writing for publications all over the world on a variety of topics that fascinated her—food, women in business, travel, wine, self-development, spirituality, design. You name it, she wrote about it. Kathryn's relentless curiosity about the world and its inhabitants made her a perfect journalist. She loved her condo in the Nob Hill district of Portland, Oregon. After her last break-up, from a man who said that he was roughly "70 percent committed" after a year together, she refashioned her condo, threw a fabulous party, and became incredibly fascinated with Pacific Northwest wines. And for a bit, all seemed right with the world. She imagined her life without her one great love and didn't pass out. Progress. She was going to be okay. She would have her work, her friends, and her adorable sister Audrey. What more could a girl want? But, after a few months, the nudging started up again. She began to feel the presence of a man — not only in her waking life, but at night in her dreams. He felt familiar, although she couldn't see his face. In that feeling existed a promise of a love she had never known before. It was back. She was being called, yet again, back to The Quest.

And that's how she ended up in front of Samorio, tears streaming down her face, goose bumps covering her body. This was it. He was right, she could feel it.

Suddenly, though, a small piece of his "prophecy" brought Kathryn back to reality.

Wait—did he say two children? Two girls? Stacy and Allison? Um, that was *so* not part of her vision. Kathryn was also untraditional in that she did not want children. It was one of those things that seemed to carry women away from themselves and their true callings in life, and she simply wasn't one of them. She had raised her little sister Audrey after their parents' divorce and felt that at 10-years-old, she had experienced all of the diaper-changing and late-night feedings she wanted to. Her mother had been forced to work three jobs, which left her little time for them. It was just her and her sister—two peas in a pod. A pod that didn't need more peas.

"Kathryn, Kathryn, did you hear me?"

She came back, focusing in on Samorio's dark, lovely features, his eyes staring inquisitively at her.

"I'm sorry, Samorio, I was drifting away for a bit there. What did you say?"

He smiled softly.

"It's to be expected, this is quite a lot to share. I would ask that you continue with the chakra meditation that I gave to you earlier to keep your energy open to receiving this Matthew. How does that feel to you?"

"It's perfect, thank you. Can I ask a question though?"

"Of course, my child. What is it?"

She gulped, her heart beating so fast, she could barely keep up. Her mind raced in a thousand different directions. In fact, parts of her mind were arguing the baby scenario—maybe she would be a good mother. Maybe Matthew already had children and she became their mother, because their real mother had been killed in some tragic accident. There were so many possibilities that she decided to forgo her current reservations over Samorio's two-child prediction. Right now, there were more important details to attend to—like this Matthew. Her mind raced trying to imagine what he looked like. Would he have dark hair, eyes, and skin—like the men she was usually drawn to? Or would he be fair-skinned with light eyes? Would his eyes search hers, looking into her soul or would it take time for him to recognize her? Whatever it was, she had to believe it would be exactly what she desired, even if she didn't know it at the time.

"How will I know when I've met him?"

For a brief moment, she caught something in Samorio's eyes. She wasn't 100 percent sure what it was, but she thought she saw his eyes twinkle. Did he know more than he was letting on?

"Oh, you'll know my dear, you'll know."

"What does that even mean?" Kathryn asked. When it came to love, Kathryn continually second-guessed herself. It exasperated her to no end. She "knew" what was best for her in her career and friends, but in love she had never had an "I just know" moment.

Samorio chuckled, and then his face turned serious.

"And Kathryn…"

"Yes?"

"It won't be easy." He closed his eyes. "But, it will be worth it."

Chapter 2

"What you seek is seeking you." –Rumi

Kathryn felt completely ungrounded after her reading with Samorio. But, she also felt validated and affirmed—the feeling that she was destined to spend her life with the other half of her soul was finally confirmed by a source outside of her head. Throughout her life, there was always this itch, this burn to meet him—her soul mate. She could never explain it, but it was such a deep yearning that she knew no matter what anyone said it was her destiny. To have this confirmed by a perfect stranger, someone so tuned in to Spirit, was a relief. It made her feel like everything was going to be okay. She hadn't been some crazy 10-year-old creating fantasies to soothe herself. Her knowing was real. Now, after her time with Samorio, she was feeling something she had never felt before—peace.

In that moment, she knew that she had wanted to find her One for a reason; it was her path. The Quest was not some silly childhood fantasy like most everyone in her life asserted—it was what she was meant to experience.

Samorio had simply confirmed what Kathryn always felt was true. And now, she had a name and a career path to look for, er, be open to. She had to remember not to force it. Forcing it could ruin everything. She was going to need help with this. Fortunately, she had Hillary and Paul, her sister Audrey, and her best friend Jess pulling for her.

Hillary and Paul got to it right away. Hillary called the day after she met with Samorio and asked if she would like to meet up with them for happy hour at their favorite spot, Portland City Grill. Located on the 30th floor in the U.S. Bank Tower, it provided spectacular views of the city, views that were impossible to find elsewhere. Of course, she couldn't say no to the sushi or fries on the happy hour menu or the Malbec for that matter (a magical combo, she was sure). Besides, she was practically bursting at the seams to tell Hillary and Paul about her reading with Samorio, and get their perspective on how she could meet her Matthew.

"So," Hillary said as she leaned over the table, the piano music drifting in around them. "Tell us, how was it? What did he say? Do you have a soul mate?"

You would have thought this was Hillary's Quest the way she so earnestly pressed Kathryn for the details. Hillary and Kathryn had become friends at a mastermind group, which met every other week, supporting one another in attracting whatever it was they were focused on. At that time, Kathryn was building her freelance writing business and set weekly goals for the stories she would get, the publications she would write for and how much money she would make each month. She had been in a hyper-focused career mode. But even so, the second she met Hillary, they both knew they would be friends forever. Kathryn remembered seeing Hillary's soft features, marine blue eyes, and loving smile, and just knowing that she was her friend. End of story. The two embraced at the end of the night saying "I love you" and laughing. They couldn't explain their connection and always joked that they must have known one another in a past life. Who else met and knew they would be lifelong friends? Um, soul mates, that's who. Proof again of its existence.

Kathryn always imagined it would be like that with her romantic soul mate. She would walk into a room and just know. Isn't that what everyone said happened anyway? God, she was really hoping that was how it went down. However, now that she had all of this information at her fingertips, she wondered if she could access that kind of peaceful place, the place that would say, "This One."

"Alright, I'll tell you. Everything. Are you ready?" Kathryn asked. She loved being able to build the tension around the news. How often did she have this kind of juicy information to share with her best friends? The waiter arrived with their sushi and fries, and they waited until he left before responding.

"Yes!" Hillary and Paul said in unison.

"So, first, thank you for recommending Samorio," Kathryn said. "He was…magical, it's like he knew exactly what I needed to know. I didn't even have to ask him. He immediately began talking about my soul mate."

"I told you!" Hillary exclaimed. "He always knows what you need."

"Exactly! So, he gave me incredible details. Get this…" she said, taking a deep breath. "He told me that my soul mate's name is Matthew, and that he will work with sustainable farms and that we'll have two children and live in Europe."

"Oh my god!" Hillary clasped her hand over her mouth.

"Wow." Paul said, nodding, not looking the least bit surprised.

Hillary grabbed Kathryn's hands. "Okay, who do we know named Matthew? We've got to think."

"I know, right?! I've been racking my brain since he told me. But so far, no one."

"Well, technically," Paul said, taking this as his opportunity to bring in some form of rational thought. "You probably don't even know this Matthew. He probably lives two blocks down from you and you've never even met him."

Hillary and Kathryn both looked a bit deflated at the thought.

"You're right," Kathryn said. "It's far more likely that I've never met him. And that means, I need to be open to allowing him into my life."

Paul nodded. "You're exactly right. Just relax and be open, and before you know it, he'll appear."

Kathryn smiled, took a sip of her Malbec, and hoped Paul was right.

◝◞

It was a week later and Kathryn was on her way to a spiritual conference to see Esther Hicks as she channeled a group of non-physical beings called Abraham. Abraham spoke exclusively about the Law of Attraction, and Kathryn had been reading their books for years. This would be her first time seeing Esther/Abraham live. Her best friend, Jess, was going with her. Kathryn could hardly wait. She was so excited to see one of her favorite authors in person that she had woken up at the crack of dawn. Besides, she had never seen someone channel non-physical entities before. She wondered if Esther would look different, sound different, or contort herself in a bizarre manner. After a couple of anxious hours, Kathryn showed up at Jess's apartment, promptly at 8 a.m., just as they had agreed.

"I'm still not ready! Come on up!" Jess yelled through the intercom.

Grrr. Kathryn could feel irritation rising within her. Since Samorio's prediction, Kathryn noticed she felt more on edge. She had the information she wanted; she just didn't know what to do with it. She was certainly hoping that spending half the day at the conference along with other high-vibrating souls would help give her the perspective she needed. Another delay to that end was not welcome. She begrudgingly climbed the stairs to Jess's apartment.

Jess already had the door wide open and her small white Maltese, Olivia, was barking up a storm in the hallway upon Kathryn's arrival.

"Kath! Yay! Oliv, hush! You'll wake all the neighbors. Come in, come in before people start screaming at us."

Jess always seemed to have more energy than anyone else in the room. Her gorgeous black curls were piled high atop her head and an exotic red scarf draped across her neck. Jess was notorious for dressing in all black, accompanied by colorful, striking accents. Whenever the two of them were out and about, people would stop to ask Jess a question or compliment her—anything. They didn't even know why they were drawn to her, they just were. And Jess knew it.

Kathryn sighed, looking down at her jeans and sweater. She was far too conservative; her sister Audrey was continually telling her that. If only she could accessorize like Jess. All she had managed for the day was big silver hoop earrings along with the silver Egyptian epitaph necklace Jess had gotten her on a trip to Egypt. She mourned that she didn't have the sense to also grab the bright blue-and-pink scarf Jess also had gotten her on the same trip.

"So, are you excited?" Jess's voice interrupted her self-imposed fashion flogging.

"If it wasn't 8 a.m., I would be bouncing off the walls. I normally would have indulged in some caffeine, but I don't want to mess up my vibration in any way. I can't *believe* we're going to see Esther channeling Abraham."

Just uttering those words snapped Kathryn back into reality. She was about to see one of her favorite authors channeling a nonphysical entity right in front of her eyes. The thought of it made her want to drag Jess out by the hair.

"Okay, hold on (Jess could usually read her mind), I just need to put on some mascara and I'll be ready to go," Jess said.

Kathryn took some time to try to settle down internally. Would she meet Matthew at the conference? She sat down on Jess's purple couch, attempting to calm herself. Incense wafted throughout the studio and she couldn't help but smile at Jess's enormous dream catcher that hung over her bed. Maybe she needed one of those to catch her Matthew. While she had been trying to keep Matthew speculation at bay, she wasn't totally successful. Everywhere she went, she found herself wondering if the man in front of her might be him. It was beginning to get ridiculous. She knew the Law of Attraction so whenever one tries to make something happen or wants something to happen intensely, that wanting energy pushes whatever it is away. The key was to relax and enjoy her life, like Paul had advised, letting the Universe bring her what she requested. She was going to attend a lecture by *the* authorities on the Law of Attraction—she needed to apply some of what she already knew. She sighed and wandered over to Jess's dining table with various self-help books strewn about.

"So, do you think you'll meet Matthew today?" Jess shouted from the bathroom. Kathryn had called Jess as she left the reading with Samorio and filled her in. While Jess wasn't much interested in finding The One for herself (she loved dating more than relation-ships), she seemed to enjoy supporting Kathryn's Quest.

Damn. How did Jess know everything she was thinking?

"Well, it's possible—isn't it? I mean, it's a spiritual conference."

"But did Samorio say Matthew was spiritual?" Jess was also good at being more of the head in their friendship. She was a Capricorn and continually grounded Kathryn's Aries fire down into reality.

"Hmm...good point, no he didn't. I guess I just assumed he would be, since it's how I live my life. Why didn't I ask him that? I swear the minute he gave me a name, location, and a career, I was so stunned I couldn't think to say anything else."

Jess stepped out of the bathroom, grabbing her bag.

"Here's the deal: if he's your soul mate, you'll know. Right? You'll just feel it?"

"God, I hope so. But, remember when I 'felt' it with Tom. What a disaster he turned out to be. He had the balls to say I was too deep. I mean, duh. Had he met me? Yes, I'm into exploring the depth of life, and yes, I get that can be annoying to someone who just wants to play video games all day, but I'm pretty sure I let people know this as soon as I meet them. Bottom line, I'm just not so sure I trust myself anymore to know."

"May I remind you," Jess stepped in close, placing her hand lovingly on Kathryn's shoulder. "That you never thought Tom was your soul mate, only a great guy to have a relationship with. And he was. For like two seconds that you then extended to six months, but you knew—didn't you—that he wasn't the One?"

Ah yes, she had a point. She also had a far better memory than Kathryn. In fact, now that she was thinking about it, she knew the exact moment when she felt with absolute certainty that Tom was not her One. They had spent the day with friends at a wine festival and had what Kathryn thought was a wonderful time. They had come back to his apartment and were laughing, telling jokes, and wrestling around. Suddenly, he said to her mid-wrestle, "You're kind of smothering. I need more space in this relationship." In that moment, her inner voice said, "Um, hello! NOT the One. Move on, please."

And so she had.

"You're right. I have to trust myself. I really do," Kathryn reasserted. "I've grown since Tom anyway—that was so 2010. Okay, I will know when I meet Matthew that he is the guy. I will just know."

"Plus, his name will be Matthew, so half the work will already be done for you."

"Right? Okay, now that we've settled that and we've lost any chance of getting a good seat to see one of my all-time favorite authors, can we please leave?"

Jess rolled her eyes, tossed her scarf behind one shoulder, and said, "Let's roll."

The walk from Jess's Southwest Portland studio to the downtown Hilton where Esther was speaking was filled with long silences followed by curses about the Oregon drizzle in June. Despite the gloomy skies, Kathryn's excitement was starting to build. Matthew was close; she could feel it. She was on her path, and as far as she could tell, she was doing all of the right things to call him in. To keep her vibration high, she was now going to see one of her favorite teachers, in an environment her soul mate was sure to be visiting. She couldn't wait to write a book about this journey. While she had spent the past five years working as a freelance writer and journalist, her ultimate dream was to write books, much like her favorite author Paulo Coelho. Kathryn dreamed of writing books that transformed people's lives the way Coelho's work had inspired her. Perhaps her love story could do just that.

They arrived at the Hilton 10 minutes before show time, much to Kathryn's delight. After a few serious minutes of scouring the hotel ballroom, she and Jess were able to score seats in the third row, not far from where Esther was speaking. Kathryn was brimming with excitement. At the end of the lecture, questions were allowed and she was hoping Esther would call on her. She wanted to know if everyone had a soul mate or if people could just partner up with whomever and make it work through sheer determination.

The lights dimmed and the lecture began.

Esther came on stage, looking radiant in black flowing pants and top. Her hair was pinned back and her skin glowed. Reportedly in her sixties, Esther didn't look a day over 40. She had a fairly high-pitched voice and moved with ease on the stage as she welcomed the 500 or so guests in attendance in the large Hilton ballroom.

"Thank you for coming. Now, good-bye."

She closed her eyes, and her head began to bob up and down. Her features started to harden, her soft oval face taking on a more square masculine look. Then, she opened her eyes and said, "Good morning." Only now her voice was that of a man's, and her face and body took on a more rigid, masculine tone.

Watching the entire transformation left Kathryn in awe.

"Good morning," Kathryn said along with the crowd, which was seated classroom style in rows of chairs facing the small stage where Esther, who was now Abraham, stood.

Esther began speaking and the information came in so quickly that Kathryn couldn't absorb it fast enough. She scribbled furiously in the small notebook she had brought, but even then it was impossible to process all of the guidance being provided. When it was time for questions, Kathryn's was one of the first hands to rise—as high as she could. She closed her eyes, visualizing her energy floating above the crowd to catch Esther's attention. Unfortunately, it didn't work. The first half of the session came to a close without the opportunity for Kathryn to ask her question. Jess squeezed her hand, turned to her and said, "She'll call on you during the next segment, don't worry."

Kathryn *was* worried; she really wanted the answer to this question and was sure Esther/Abraham would have it. But, without having any control over the outcome, Kathryn would have to surrender. She reminded herself that the only thing she could do was trust the process. If Kathryn and the world were meant to know the truth about soul mates, Esther would call on her or call on someone with the same question. For now, it was intermission and she had bigger things to take care of. Like peeing.

Kathryn had been drinking water like crazy to keep her energy field clear and well-hydrated (she hypothesized that maybe *that* would allow for her to get called on). Apparently, one aspect of her clear energy plan worked, because it was moving through her at a rapid rate and it was all she could think about while pushing through the throngs of people to the nearest restroom. She grabbed Jess and the two headed for the bathrooms. As they walked into the ballroom lobby area, there were scores more people milling about, looking at books and CDs. Suddenly, a man in a gray suit caught Kathryn's eye. He was sitting in front of the American Marketing Association conference entrance with two other men, but his eyes were fixed on her. At first, she thought he must be looking at someone else. Her brown curly hair was huge thanks to the Oregon humidity and rain, and her simple off-white sweater and purple tank couldn't have drawn that much attention, especially when paired with jeans and black Danskos. She looked back again and there he was, staring at her, only this time he was smiling. She smiled back and felt a hot rush through her abdomen.

While waiting in the bathroom line, she couldn't get his face out of her head. His golden skin, strong jaw line, and aqua blue eyes were inviting. His smile was big, strong, and confident. She liked how he felt—even from afar. She smoothed her hair in the bathroom mirror—doing what she could to avoid noticing the horrible effect of the fluorescent lights on her skin. While silently cursing the inventor of fluorescents, she quickly put her hair back into a low side bun, pulling a few strands out at the sides to soften the look. This time, she was ready to smile his way more confidently. Perhaps he would come over and introduce himself.

On her way out of the bathroom, he caught her eye right away—as if he was looking for her. She smiled and felt the heat rush through her, this time in her lower belly. He was in her second chakra all right—the center of sexuality and sensuality. It was crazy. She felt like she was 16 years old, she was turned on and nervous, all at the same time. To the outside world, though, she was barely aware of the strikingly handsome man who kept staring her way. She and Jess walked casually over to an area in the lobby that was a safe enough distance away from him and stood talking. Kathryn made sure she was facing the mystery man's direction.

"So, is he looking?" Jess whispered, even though they were about

20 feet away from him. Kathryn had clued her in when they were in the bathroom.

"I can't tell, your hair is in the way."

Jess's black curls were out of control and blocking Kathryn's vision, so all she could see was one of the other men sitting at the table.

Jess slowly rocked her weight onto her other hip, like a real pro.

"How 'bout now?"

"Yep, he's watching—trying to pretend like he's interested in whatever that other guy is talking about."

"Why don't you just go over there and say, 'Hey, I'm Kathryn, is your name Matthew by chance?'"

"Um, like that wouldn't scare the shit out of him. No. Besides, I want him to come after me. I'm not chasing him."

And just like that, as if he knew her very thoughts, he came over.

"Hi. I'm Scott. What are you all learning in there?"

And just like that, he was merely another guy trying to get her number.

"Oh, hi. Yeah, I'm Kathryn. And we're not learning much, just having our lives transformed, that's all." Suddenly, she was sassy.

She gave him a half smile. Scott? Ugh. She didn't feel any need to turn on the charm since he clearly was not her man. Kathryn looked around for Jess to be her wing woman, but somehow, she had disappeared. Hadn't she heard that his name was Scott? There was no need to bother, in fact, maybe Jess would like to go out with him.

"I couldn't help noticing you and your smile. It's gorgeous."

"Oh, thank you so much—that's really sweet."

And it was. Kathryn had to remind herself that it wasn't his fault he wasn't her Matthew.

Just then, the gong rang; intermission was ending.

"Oh, that's for me, I've got to head back. You should come in— it's incredible—Esther Hicks is channeling Abraham and it's totally life-changing."

"Abraham, eh? Sounds interesting. I've never heard of him."

No surprise there. Kathryn tried not to roll her eyes.

"Well, do you have a card?" Scott asked.

"No, not on me. Sorry."

"Can I give you my phone number?"

Kathryn turned to walk away; she wasn't about to miss any moment of Esther channeling Abraham.

"I don't have my cell on me and I'm not good at memorizing numbers. But, it was nice to meet you." She smiled, and hurried back into the auditorium.

Once settled back in, she dismissed Scott from her memory, along with the shot of heat and butterflies that had enveloped her when she looked into his eyes. She grabbed Jess's hand, gave it a squeeze and the two smiled at one another. Jess leaned in and whispered, "She's going to call on you; I know it."

But, Abraham didn't choose Kathryn. She couldn't quite understand it; her question was one she had never heard before. Do soul mates really exist? Was that so hard to answer? Apparently, it was, because Kathryn had read all of the Abraham books and listened to every CD she could get her hands on, and she still didn't know the answer.

And, because Kathryn needed everything to have a reason, she used her powers of deduction based on what she heard in the lecture and surmised that according to the principles of Law of Attraction, if she wanted to create a soul mate in her experience, she could. In fact, according to the Law of Attraction, Kathryn (and anyone) could attract anything she wanted into her life: soul mate, successful career as a novelist, a house at the beach and in the city—whatever. She simply had to believe she could. During the closing meditation, she took a deep breath, sank into her heart, and asked if a soul mate union was what was in her highest good to manifest.

⟡

As she and Jess left the workshop, they skipped through the hotel lobby, feeling light as a feather. Kathryn planned to spend the rest of the day relaxing, letting the messages from she had received at the seminar wash over her. As they opened the door to head back out into the real world, the Portland rain fell in even larger drops. But, even it couldn't dampen Kathryn and Jess's spirits. They looked at each other and laughed, stopping under the hotel awning to put on their rain jackets. From behind they heard a voice.

"So, did Abraham teach you anything good?"

Kathryn abruptly turned around. Scott was standing right next to her, his bright smile making its way into her heart.

Caught off guard, she stumbled with her words.

"Um, yeah. We learned a lot." She turned to Jess and shrugged. Jess smiled back and turned around, finding something incredibly interesting on a nearby poster to focus on.

"It's weird how we keep running into each other today, isn't it?" Scott raised his left eyebrow playfully.

"Well, actually, yes, it is. We must have a message for each other. I've recently lost a pair of earrings. Do you happen to know where they might be?" She teased.

"Oh, a message? Hmm…no I don't think I have one about your earrings. You got one for me?" Now he was baiting her.

"I'm not good with messages on the spot…"

"Or memorizing phone numbers, yes, I'm starting to develop a list of items you're not incredibly savvy with."

She blushed. He was funny *and* persistent. Weren't those two qualities she really dug in a man?

"This time though," she said rather slowly as she reached into her purse. "I'm not going to let the moment pass. Everyone who comes into our life does so for a reason. So, here's my card. E-mail me or text when you have my message and then I'll give you yours."

"Impressive. I would love that."

He turned over her card, rubbing it gently with his thumb. "Live your truth," he murmured, reading the tagline off of her card.

Kathryn felt goose bumps cover her whole body and a rush of energy enter in through the top of her crown. She scratched her head to compensate. This rarely happened unless something important was occurring. What was going on? His name was Scott. Hadn't the Universe given her the name of her guy? Perhaps Scott would become an important business partner, she mused.

"Well, Scott, it was a pleasure running into you—again. You should check out Esther Hicks and Abraham sometime—you might learn something. In the meantime, I'll be waiting for my message from you."

She shook his hand and relaxed. The warmth of his hand was soothing and grounding. She felt herself stand up straighter as she smiled at him. He smiled back. He didn't release her hand. The two of them stood underneath the hotel awning, the rain dropping all around them, smiling at one another. Suddenly, he realized he still had her hand in his, and let go.

"See you soon Kathryn."

She thought it was an odd thing to say. They hadn't made any plans. But, perhaps he was being hopeful.

Kathryn grabbed Jess by the arm, and Jess turned to Scott and said, "Nice to meet you!"

Kathryn kept her eyes focused forward, but after a few minutes she couldn't help herself and looked back. When she did, she saw Scott standing there, the hotel door half open, smiling at her.

Chapter 3

"*People, since the beginning of time, have always tried to understand the universe through love.*" –*Paulo Coelho*

Kathryn tried to ignore the image of Scott's face in her mind. She tried not to check her phone or e-mail over the past few days since meeting him to see if he had reached out to her. She didn't understand what the Universe was up to. She was looking for Matthew. Meeting a man named Scott was not part of the plan. She had Samorio's prophecy and the Law of Attraction working in her favor—she could not get distracted.

Just then, her phone beeped. New text. Unknown number.

"So, I have your message. Ready? Here it is: Sometimes it's not what you think."

Whoa. That was actually helpful. Maybe Scott was *not* what she thinks. The heat, the butterflies—that could all mean something totally different. Maybe she met Scott to confirm what Samorio had said: it was Matthew she was looking for. Perhaps Scott was meant to be a friend on the spiritual path. Already she was feeling less anxious.

She took a few moments to sit and think about her message for him.

It didn't take long before one popped in. She grabbed her phone to text him back.

"That's actually helpful. Thank you! Here's yours: Trust yourself. You're right."

Kathryn took a deep breath; she didn't know what he was right about or why she was telling a perfect stranger to trust himself, but she did it anyway. She had learned over the past few years that those pop-ins, instinctual nudges, and the sometimes annoying, but repetitive, reminders all meant the same thing: follow them and you will find a piece of your bliss!

Jess made Kathryn promise that she would text back as soon as she heard from Scott, so she did, forwarding on his message. She immediately heard back (Jess was a lightning-speed text-er) with a "Yay!" along with an invite to have lunch with a group of folks from one of her coaching mastermind groups.

Everyone seemed to know Jess in her work as a highly sought-after executive coach. She worked with CEOs of large corporations all over the nation, and was paid to speak at conferences on topics like communication, business development, and the like. In the last few years, as she began to explore the spiritual side of herself, she had added to it by taking on topics like the importance of authenticity, connection, and using intuition in business. Kathryn had loved watching her grow—both as a woman and in her business. The two had shared many late-night phone calls and weekend retreats exploring the possibilities of the Universe, and how to make it work in their own lives, as well as how to better tap into their intuition.

Kathryn always enjoyed meeting new people—she never knew who they might be. Maybe she'd meet someone who was writing a book and needed a ghostwriter. Coaches were always looking for the next book to write or product to sell. Jess was kind to introduce her as, "The best writer you'll ever meet."

As Kathryn got ready to head out the door, she checked her

phone one last time (she would *not* obsess about Scott responding to her message! Or at least that's what she kept telling herself.), threw on her favorite black-and-white polka dot summer dress and black heels, and headed out to lunch at Portland's Veritable Quandary, or the VQ as the locals called it.

Unfortunately, lunch wasn't attended by anyone she didn't already know. There were about 10 of the usual suspects who were often at the events Jess hosted. Kathryn settled in with quinoa and summer veggies, along with a glass of Kendall Jackson Chardonnay. Maybe she would get some sparks for a new poem or article by sitting in on the group. She must be there for some reason she told herself. Kathryn had long ago given up the notion that randomness or coincidences occurred. The more she noticed the seeming "coincidences" in her life, the more she started to notice a common thread. Looking back even further allowed her to see that one "coincidence" led to another and another, which always seemed to lead her to something powerful—whether it was a new person in her life, new information, or just a rockin' good time. It was during instances like these that she tried to remind herself of this truth. There would be something for her here, she just had to be open to receiving it and relax enough to have a good time.

Suddenly, a name caught her attention, bringing her back into the present moment.

"And then she said, 'Now, Matthew Alan Johnson, I have told you time and time again to water the plants twice a day!' I just laughed. I'm a 25-year-old man, I know how to take care of plants. I swear, I am never housesitting for my mother again!"

Jess and the others roared with laughter. Apparently, this guy was a good storyteller.

Kathryn had never paid much attention to him, to this Matthew. She had seen him at some of Jess's events and had exchanged pleasantries with him, but nothing more. He simply wasn't her type—he wore his dirty blond hair in a slight faux-hawk, wore trendy, name-brand clothes, and it appeared that he either visited a tanning bed regularly or was getting spray tanned. Not to mention he was 25 to her 30. The last time she dated a younger man, she ended up "hanging out" at his place while he played video games. She had promised Hillary and Paul she would never do that again. Not her thing. No, this guy belonged in a nightclub with a bunch of twenty-somethings. Come to think of it, he had spent several years working in nightclubs and had only recently entered the world of self-development as a coach.

Only now, Kathryn could not take her eyes off of him.

Of course, his full name was Matthew. He had always been introduced to her as Matt and she had never given him any thought beyond that. Now, she *had* to know him. Maybe he was far more interesting than she imagined. Maybe the tan, faux-hawk, and designer clothes were just a cover for a deeper, more spiritually tuned in man.

Kathryn nudged Jess.

"Hey, so his name is Matthew?" She spoke just above a whisper, mouthing the words very carefully.

"OMG!" Jess slapped her hand to her mouth. "Could he be *your* Matthew?"

"I have no idea, but I have to find out. He's sitting clear across the table. Can you help me get over there?"

"Of course. Watch this."

Jess leaned in over the table to get the attention of Claire who was sitting next to Matthew.

"Hey Claire, I am *dying* to hear all about your new audio product. Can you switch places with Kathryn so I can get the full scoop?"

Claire didn't even hesitate.

And so it was. Kathryn thanked the Universe for blessing her with such an incredible friend and for giving her the opportunity to sit next to her potential soul mate. Okay, that was probably jumping the gun, but Kathryn couldn't help it—she was excited. She loved it when life surprised her like this.

As she sat down, Matthew gave her a slight smile, watching as she maneuvered into the chair next to him.

"So, Matthew…"

"It's Matt, really. Only my mom calls me Matthew. Or women when they're screaming my name." He winked.

Kathryn winced. He is 25, he is 25, he is 25—she reminded herself as though it were a mantra.

"Yeah, I didn't know you had family that lived in the area."

"Oh yeah, I try not to see them too often, but sometimes it happens. I just told the best and only story I have about my mother. So, let's talk about something else. How about you? How is the writing and editing going?"

"I love it. I feel super fortunate to do work I love, and work from home."

Matt raised his eyebrows, looking at her intently. She continued.

"Right now, I'm working on a piece about soul mates," she lied. "And I'm especially curious about how men feel about the concept. Women seem, in general, more open to the possibility."

Matthew looked into Kathryn's eyes and leaned in. He settled into his seat before clearing his throat .

"I actually feel we do have soul mates, but I've never met mine and I'm not even sure I would know it if I did. Maybe I won't ever meet her—I'm not sure. If I'm meant to in this life, then surely I will. But if not, that's okay, too. I suspect women are more open to the soul mate concept because women, in general, are more in touch with their intuition and spirituality. Men's egos or conditioning tend to get in the way of these things." He smiled, a bit slyly.

Kathryn was surprised. He was more intelligent than she expected.

"I agree with your assessment of female versus male when it comes to soul mates. But in order for the two to come together, men have to be willing to open up more to the process. I like to fantasize that we will just know when we meet the right person for us, but I think it depends on how much work we've done on ourselves, so we can clearly identify him or her."

He watched her carefully as she spoke.

"Hmm...agreed. What's your slant for this piece?"

This piece, what piece? Kathryn was so lost in expressing her thoughts and hearing his that she forgot she had said she was conducting research for an article.

"Oh well, I'm still developing that part. I think it will be about what we're discussing here—men and women's different viewpoints about the existence of soul mates."

"You're deeper than I initially assessed."

Matthew had completely changed the subject. Kathryn gulped. Something was happening here. Was he *The One?*

"Well, I would have to say the same about you."

"Fair enough." He smiled more fully now. Even so, his dark brown eyes remained unaffected. "I want to take you out to dinner. What do you think?"

Direct. So much easier. Maybe this was how it worked when a girl meets the guy an African psychic told her could possibly be The One. Or not. But Kathryn was game either way.

"I would enjoy that."

"Good. Me too. What's your number?"

Kathryn looked over at Jess who was pretending to be interested in an audio tele-seminar series, but was secretly watching Kathryn and Matthew interact the entire time. Jess gave her a big smile when she saw Matthew pulling out his phone and getting Kathryn's number.

∿

Dinner with Matthew, er Matt (although secretly and maybe not so secretly she would continue to call him Matthew. It was prophesized!), would take place two days from their lunch meeting on a Tuesday evening. He picked out one of her favorite wine bars, Thirst on the waterfront, and the plan was to take part in a small tasting and order a variety of appetizers.

The evening finally arrived—warmer and clearer than a typical June in Portland—and Kathryn found it hard to be herself. For some reason, she was more edgy about the date than normal. He was so bright and shiny. Spray tanned with name-brand clothes? Kathryn had clothing she had been wearing for 10 years. They were in good shape and color of course, but she was more likely to be seen shopping at the Here We Go Again consignment shop than at Juicy Couture. And he was so young, she thought despondently as she peered in the mirror at her crow's feet.

She must have checked her reflection more than a dozen times, smoothing her brown locks and re-assessing her black-and-white capris with strappy black sandals and white sweater set. She was beyond nervous. It had been about a month since her last date and this one felt even more intense with Samorio's Matthew prophecy. Kathryn took one last look in the mirror and sighed. At 5'6, her 120-lbs. frame sometimes worked for her and other times didn't. But, it was what she had—she had to remind herself. She needed to relax, examining her flaws in the mirror was not helping. And being insecure was not serving her either. She had to trust that everything was happening as it should. So, she thanked the Universe out loud for her body, grabbed her purse, and headed out for her first date with Matthew.

As she walked up the waterfront, Kathryn saw Matthew already seated at a table outside near the water. He looked absolutely at ease in his black slacks and black button button-up dress shirt. He stood up as she approached the table.

"Kathryn, you look lovely. Thank you for making it tonight. On time, no less." He checked his watch and smiled back at her approvingly.

"Er, oh, I didn't know I was on clock watch. But, you're welcome. Thanks for getting us this great table by the water."

Matthew pulled out her chair and she sat down. It was a perfect summer evening and she took a deep breath while taking in the scenery around them. Birds flew overhead, as people walked the waterfront.

"We're really blessed to live here, aren't we?" Matthew said.

"I was just thinking that exact thing. It is so beautiful here."

"Well, I hope you don't mind, but I took the liberty of ordering us a couple of appetizers and glasses of Malbec."

Kathryn smiled.

"You did your research, very impressive. Thank you."

She couldn't believe he was so attentive, maybe dating younger men wasn't such a bad thing after all.

As the wine and food arrived, Matthew and Kathryn discussed their current careers and their love for Portland, as well as their passion for food and wine. Kathryn let the wine warm her from the inside out, causing her body to relax. Eventually, the conversation settled into talk about dream careers and their ultimate vision for their lives.

Kathryn shared her desire to one day make a living as a full-time novelist, traveling the world with her words, and inspiring others to live out their dreams. She wanted her books to remind people of who they really were. Matthew watched her curiously as she spoke, nodding his head in obvious approval and understanding of her dream. She felt closer to him being able to share this side of herself and found herself talking much longer than she normally would about the places she hoped to visit, how she would like to use the millions she would make (first on a three-month trip around the world, then real estate investments, paying for college for her yet unborn nieces and nephews, and finally starting a foundation for micro-credit lending programs in less-fortunate countries). Matthew seemed to understand Kathryn's belief that everyone came into the world to accomplish a personal dream—whatever that might be. He nodded in agreement when Kathryn shared that she felt each individual brought unique gifts with him or her, and it was up to each person to put those gifts out into the world.

It had been a very long time since Kathryn had shared these beliefs with a man, on a date. Typically she focused in on the other person, always asking questions, and never fully opening up. But with Matthew, he was receptive and she liked that. However, once she realized she had been talking so much, she felt slightly embarrassed, even though Matthew seemed engaged and interested in everything she shared. She quickly apologized, ordered a glass of Rose City Red and focused in on Matthew.

"So, now that you've heard about my ever-so detailed life fantasy, tell me about yours. Where do you see yourself in the future?"

He paused, picking up his cloth napkin to dab his mouth of red wine and said, "I don't usually share this with people, but since you've been so incredibly generous in sharing your vision, I will do the same. But, first I have to preface it by saying, please don't laugh."

"I wouldn't!"

"Well, I've always dreamed of living abroad in Europe and managing local farms. I would really love to specialize in sustainable farming technology and make a difference in the world that way. I know it seems crazy and totally out of left field—I'm a coach for god's sake, but if I'm honest with myself, that's really what I want to do."

Kathryn could not believe her ears. She was stunned. The outside world seemed to evaporate as Matthew came into her full vision. THIS IS HIM. The Quest is OVER! I have found him. Samorio was right! Matthew, however, was awaiting her response. The waitress appeared at just the right time with her glass of red, giving her the extra time she needed to return to the present moment. She cleared her throat, smiled at him ever so lovingly (as she imagined what in the world their children—that she wasn't even sure she wanted—would look like) and spoke.

"That isn't funny at all. It's actually quite noble of you. From nightclubs to self-development to sustainable farming. Now that's an evolution to be proud of."

Matthew raised his glass, "And so, I propose a toast." Kathryn raised her glass as well, beaming from ear to ear.

"To evolutions to be proud of."

"Salut."

And so it was.

After a walk along the waterfront discussing their views on spirituality (he had a more Buddhist philosophy, while Kathryn preferred an integration of all the traditions), the evening was coming to a close. The sun had set and a slight breeze picked up over the water. They both stood, staring out at the city lights and the Willamette River, suddenly silent, taking the whole evening in.

Matthew stood beside her, his arm touching hers. As the breeze blew, Kathryn felt a rush of energy from her crown to her toes. She was loving Matthew's energy and their exchanges throughout the evening. All of her former negative thoughts about him had vanished. She felt peaceful.

Matthew broke the silence.

"I had the most wonderful time with you tonight Kathryn," he said in a low voice, turning to face her.

A waft of her hair blew up into her face. He reached out gently and pushed it back.

"You have been quite a surprise, one that I'm grateful for."

His hand lingered a bit longer on her cheek. She didn't move; she was totally entranced. He spoke slowly, softly, as if he knew what was coming next, but wanted to hold the moment in his hands for as long as possible.

"I look forward to our further exploration. You are a beautiful, passionate woman. And I have a feeling we have some things to teach one another."

Very gingerly, he moved his face closer to hers. The wind took hold of her hair, and once again he lifted his hands to move it gently from her face. Only this time, he didn't take his eyes off of her. He held her gaze, both of his hands on either side of her jaw, as he came closer to her lips.

"I'm wondering…"

"Yes," she breathed.

"If you would like me…" His lips were almost touching hers. "…to kiss you."

She smiled, staring deeply into the chocolaty pools of his brown eyes.

Just then, his lips touched hers, slowly and tenderly, as his hands caressed her face. He moved his head to the other side and this time used his tongue to gently enter her mouth. Kathryn obliged, soaking in the moment—the wind in her hair, his hands on her face, and his tongue in her mouth. This moment was one she was certain she would never forget.

He pulled back, smiling at her.

He quickly kissed her freckled nose and put his arm around her.

"Let's get you safely back home, my dear."

For a moment, Kathryn had forgotten all about home. Or time or space.

"Oh yes!" She grabbed her cell phone checking the time. "I've got 15 minutes until the streetcar arrives—I've got to hurry."

"I'll get you there in time, let's go!"

With that, he grabbed her hand as they ran through Waterfront Park in the hopes of catching the streetcar. She screamed playfully as they ran through the park hand in hand, and he laughed along with her. Their combined energy was making them both feel giddy.

They arrived at the streetcar just as it pulled up.

Kathryn stopped and turned to face Matthew. There was really nothing more to say. He was here.

"Thank you," she said, and with that she blew him a kiss and hopped onto the streetcar.

As it pulled away, all that could be seen was Kathryn's bright, beaming face.

Chapter 4

"One often meets their destiny on the way to somewhere else. At first glance it may appear too hard. Look again. Always look again."
—Maryanne Radmacher

Kathryn could not wait to meet with Samorio and tell him her amazingly good news. In just a matter of weeks, she had met her Matthew and begun dating him. She was being given the gift to her lifelong Quest—she had met her soul mate. The very soul mate she was prophesized to meet only weeks earlier. Kathryn felt like she was living in a dream.

Samorio looked surprised to see her when she popped by unexpectedly late one afternoon. Kathryn had wrapped up edits on a boring science-based book on insect reproduction and couldn't wait to get out of her home office to focus on something far more interesting—her love life. Samorio was sitting outside on the front porch of the home where he held his spiritual practice. It looked as though he had a glass of ice tea in his hands as he rocked back and forth on the porch swing.

"Well, Kathryn, how are you? What brings you here?"

"Samorio, you'll never believe what has happened since I last saw you."

"I feel I might, my dear."

"I met him! I met Matthew."

Samorio suddenly looked very serious. He raised his eyes up to the clouds and then looked back down at Kathryn. He got up and opened the door to enter his office.

"Come in, I have a few minutes before my next client arrives."

She was confused. Why wasn't he jumping up and down with her?

Samorio led Kathryn into his office; a cozy room filled with an eclectic mix of African art, a Buddha, a red-and-white Asian lantern and a set of soft beige chairs in front of a large, maple wood desk. Sage incense burned on the altar and Kathryn took in a deep breath. She loved the smell. It was the smell of possibility. She often lit sage in her home, before and after anyone entered, and in the evenings to keep the energy in her home balanced. It was a smell that reminded her of peace and spirit—all at once.

"I thought…I thought you'd be excited for me Samorio. What's with the frown?" Kathryn teased.

Slowly, Samorio smiled. He put his hands together, as if to pray, looking up at her from behind his large desk.

"My dear Kathryn, are you really sure you want to date someone who is so closely tied to your friends? Isn't this Matthew quite close with your best friend's friends?"

His frown was now replaced with a curious smile.

"Um, what does that matter? His name is Matthew and he wants to run sustainable farms in Europe—what else do I need to know here? And besides, how did you know I met him through my best friend?"

Samorio's smile broadened.

"I had a feeling, let's just say that. Are you telling me that you're sure that this Matthew is *the* Matthew that Spirit told me would be your husband?"

"I am completely sure. It's not like there are a ton of Matthews wandering around with the same dream of farming in Europe who happen to be attracted to me and interested in taking me out on dates."

Well, the taking her on dates part wasn't entirely true. Matthew hadn't paid on their first date, they had gone dutch. And while that had been a little disappointing to Kathryn (she loved it when a man paid for the first date—it was a romantic gesture in her eyes), she hadn't bothered worrying about it. She couldn't really be *that* nitpicky could she? This was The One, so maybe he would eventually come around to treating her every so often. Besides, Samorio was getting her off track—she had met a man with the exact qualifications he had predicted. Shouldn't he be high-fiving her and the Buddha or something?

She continued on.

"Samorio, the way he came into my life was totally unexpected. You know how everyone says, when you least expect it, blah, blah, blah? Turns out, I think they might be right. It took me totally by surprise; he was there—right in front of my face! I had even met him before, but never thought anything of it. I mean, really, when does that happen?"

Kathryn was a bit exasperated with Samorio. He had given her this gift—information she had been curious about her entire life. And now, she had done it; she had found him, and here Samorio was questioning the validity of her Matthew. It seemed totally irrational. Kathryn had simply assumed that Samorio would have been more supportive of her good news.

"My dear Kathryn, I wish you well on this next phase of your journey. You do know what is best for you. I just wanted to check to see if you were sure."

Kathryn was irritated, and felt the sudden urge to leave. Psychics were so frustrating. One minute up in the clouds, the next a concerned parent. She wanted to celebrate, not poke holes in her wondrous good fortune.

"Thanks for your time, considering I showed up unannounced. I will let you know how it goes. I feel really blessed to have received the reading from you and then to meet a man who matches the description you gave me. I can't wait to find out what happens next!"

She pasted on her favorite fake smile, gave Samorio a hug and dashed out of his office. She wasn't going to let his less-than-supportive attitude get in her way. As she walked down SE Division to her black Toyota Prius, she smiled. No one could stop her now, she had finished her Quest. And who knew what the future would hold for her? In five to 10 years, she could be living on a sustainable farm in Europe. With children. The children part was still a bit terrifying, and if she was really going to be popping out someone's babies, she was going to need more like 15 years before going to Europe—but whatever. The point was, it was happening. Samorio had given her the key and now she needed to move forward with it.

Despite her trepidation about having Matthew's babies, she did know one thing for sure: she wasn't going to need to see a psychic ever again. In less than a week, Kathryn was going to Brazil to see John of God with one of her mentors, Ovida. Ovida had been to Abadiania, Brazil, to see the great healer John of God many times. In fact, she spoke fluent Portuguese. Ovida had agreed to let Kathryn come along, so she could practice serving as a guide for someone who had never been to see John of God before. Kathryn was eager to have a radically different spiritual experience and tap into her intuition to a greater degree. Soon, she would be so tuned in to Source, Spirit, her higher self—or whatever it was that Samorio accessed—that it would no longer be necessary for her to ask anyone else about her future.

She was lost in these thoughts as she opened the door of her Prius, when someone caught her eye. She squinted to be sure. No, it couldn't be. But yes, in fact, it was. Right across the street from her was Scott, having dinner with a group of people she had never seen before at a small Indian café. She pursed her lips together, trying to figure out what to do next. He was most likely going to see her. Should she go over there? Should she jump in her car?

Kathryn took far too long staring in his direction, as her mind strategically tried to justify this synchronistic occurrence. As if he could feel her eyes on him, he looked over in her direction in the most natural way. And without a bit of surprise, Scott smiled and waved. Startled, Kathryn's hand flailed up in some type of wave and she shouted "Hey!" and then, totally embarrassed, jumped into her car. She managed to hit her head as she did so. She felt like a complete idiot. What was wrong with her? What was with the flailing wave and shouting? There was something about their connection that caught her off guard. Scott was everywhere. And he was charming and attractive. But, he was not The One and Kathryn did not want to get distracted. She was not about to let anything deter her; she had to focus.

As she drove back home, her mind began to spin over the possible meanings for the synchronicities that were occurring between she and Scott. But with Matthew in her life and her trip to Brazil just days away, she couldn't indulge the tugging inside of her. Damn him, she thought silently, why won't he just go away? Suddenly, her phone rang—it was her sister Audrey.

"Hey Kat, I want details on your Matthew!"

Audrey was an incredibly in-demand stylist and Kathryn practically had to book two to three weeks in advance to get any time with her—even though she was her sister. Fortunately, the Universe had created texting, which was how they primarily communicated. She had sent a few ecstatic texts off to Audrey after her first date with Matthew, with Audrey responding with a flood of "OMG!" "CAN'T WAIT"s and the like. Audrey was pretty much the only one who called her Kat—only family and very, very close friends ever called her that. Kathryn liked it that way—it felt more intimate and special to her.

"It's so good to hear from you Aud. Tell me when you have your next opening and I can give you all of the details."

"Well, actually…I was wondering if I could stop by your place tonight. I really need to have you review this press release I'm putting together about a new line of cosmetics and hair care that I'm bringing into the salon. So, I figured we could kill two birds with one stone—I could hear all about your soul mate and you could edit my release. What do you think? I'll bring some Malbec and dark chocolate to sweeten the deal…"

Kathryn rarely, if ever, could say "no" to her sister.

"Of course, I'll be home in 15."

"Perfect! I'll be over in 20."

True to form, Audrey arrived right on time with one of Kathryn's favorite Malbec's and a Trader Joe's organic dark chocolate bar. She also looked like she had just walked out of an *InStyle* magazine photo shoot. Her chin-length blonde tresses were beautifully styled; straight with a slight curve to her chin. Her blue eyes shone like the bright waters of the Caribbean and her outfit—my god, Kathryn thought, where does she get this stuff?—consisted of knee-high brown suede boots that were the perfect complement to her form-fitting jeans and caramel off-the-shoulder top. Paired with a long gold chain and Chanel gold hoops, Audrey was breathtaking. At 7 p.m. on a Tuesday, no less. Kathryn looked down at her usual workout gear and smiled. How could two people be so different, yet be from the same blood line?

Audrey, however, didn't seem to notice any of this. If she was aware of the huge dissonance in their clothing for the evening, she didn't do anything to show it beyond an attempt to smooth Kathryn's hair into a stylish bun (from the ponytail it was in). She quickly gave up, and said, "You really need to make an appointment with me," and then moved the conversation on. Kathryn was about to point out that she had unsuccessfully tried to make an appointment with her, but quickly closed her mouth. It wasn't worth the battle and they had other, more important, topics to cover.

"Okay, first thing's first Kat, I have to know about this Matthew. The very Matthew that Samorio predicted you would meet Amazing!"

Audrey opened up the wine, gracefully poured it into two huge wine glasses, while Kathryn grabbed the chocolate bar and began moving their conversation into the living room. Kathryn had to admit, telling the story was a lot of fun. It reminded her of the magic she so believed in and knew would one day be hers. Well, actually, the magic that was already hers.

They entered her living area decorated with a plush white area rug, comfy nude sofa, and a wine-colored accent wall. Local art graced her condo; much of it inspirational, including many of MaryAnne Radmacher's pieces. She also had her corner altar set up with her Buddha, crystals, incense, angel cards, worry jar (to write down and deposit her worries as they arose), and angel sculptures. She had created it with the intention of setting the tone of her home as a healing oasis, and that's exactly what her friends and family always noted whenever they came to visit. Even Audrey—who had completely different taste—continually commented on how good the space felt to her.

Now, with wine in hand, Kathryn began to relay the story in much detail to Audrey. Audrey nodded attentively, taking it all in. She had a little trouble hearing about the kiss (Kathryn was so much of a mother figure that the thought of her being engaged in any sexual activity seemed to send Audrey over the edge), but it was far too sexy to leave out, so Kathryn shared it all.

When she finished, Audrey reached over, grabbed her hand

and said, "You did it Kat. You followed the signs and the Universe brought him right into your life."

"I know! It's so magical *and* so totally unbelievable."

"So, are you guys like texting all day long? Talking on the phone whenever you aren't seeing each other?"

Kathryn paused.

"We're not 21, Aud. He has important work that he does all day and so do I."

"Wait, you haven't heard from him?"

The truth was, Kathryn hadn't heard from Matthew since that first magical date. It was going on five days now and not so much as a text from him had graced her presence.

"Well. Hmm…no. I know, it is kind of weird. But maybe when it's your soul mate, you just know and you don't have to talk all the time."

"Do you know when you'll see him again?" Audrey asked, this time with a suspicious tone in her voice.

"I know I'll see him again. I mean, of course I will—our connection was amazing. I'm sure I'll hear from him soon, very, very soon."

"Like before you leave in a few days for Brazil? Does he even know you're going?" Audrey was playing detective now.

Kathryn gulped. It hadn't really come up in conversation. She was so enthralled with Matthew and having found him, leaving the country for a couple of weeks had completely slipped her mind.

And just then, as if the gods were watching, Kathryn's phone beeped. She had a text.

"See, that's probably him now," she said (her fingers crossed).

She got up and grabbed her phone, looking back uneasily at Audrey. She hoped it was from Matthew. Not hearing from him was starting to make her a bit nervous, and Audrey's pressing only made it worse. The message, however, was not from Matthew. It was from Scott.

"Sorry you had to run out so quickly tonight. It was great seeing you—even if from just across the street. Let's hang out sometime soon, okay? Goodnight."

Ugh. Seriously, why did Scott keep showing up, Kathryn wondered. "Go away!" she silently yelled at the phone. She then quickly deleted the text.

Audrey called over, "Was it him?"

"No, just a stupid text marketer."

Matthew *did* contact her the following day via e-mail to set up their next date. They were going to Olive or Twist in the Pearl district that night and she had the perfect dress to wear. She forwarded the text to Audrey (along with details on the dress/hair/makeup for approval) to show her that while he may not have been following what Audrey thought he should do, things were definitely moving forward. Kathryn often hoped that one day she could show her sister what a loving, healthy relationship looked like. Neither of her parents had managed to have that kind of romantic relationship and as the big sister Kathryn felt like it was her responsibility.

And finally, she was going to have a chance to do just that with her soul mate, Matthew.

Kathryn applied the finishing touches to her makeup before racing out the door—dark purple eye shadow with a thick sweeping line of midnight black liquid mascara, followed by two full applications of Maybelline's Great Lash in Very Black. This, paired with a silver, strapless sheath dress and her hair curled in soft, loose waves, was sure to get Matthew's attention. She was meeting him at 8 p.m. and needed to leave right away to make it there in time. Per usual, Kathryn had waited until the final second to leave. Despite her best intentions, she usually ran five minutes late to most everything. Hopefully Matthew wouldn't be keeping track of the time on this date.

As she headed out of her apartment, she noticed her opened and half-filled suitcase. She had two more days before her big trip and she hadn't even finished packing. She just couldn't get excited about the trip since meeting Matthew. Originally, going to Brazil was an opportunity for her to connect with her higher self and Source more closely. And while she was still drawn to having this experience, since meeting Matthew, her desire for two weeks with a healer in the middle of the Amazon had waned. For now, she was content to focus on the present. With that, she added one small fix to her hair, pulling back a long front layer from the left side and securing it with a bobby pin, for that nice girl-next-door look (despite her sexy get-up) and headed out the door.

She arrived at Olive or Twist at 8:05 p.m., but didn't see Matthew in the lounge. It seemed strange since he had been so focused on being punctual for their first date, although she was grateful he wouldn't notice that she was late. She grabbed a seat on one of the gray leather couches and ordered her signature drink while she waited—a Chopin vodka and soda with lime. Minutes after ordering, Matthew arrived. He was freshly shaven and his skin beamed a golden tan tone—for some odd reason—decked out in what appeared to be a three-piece suit. Kathryn counted quickly in her head: vest, one piece; pants, two pieces; jacket over arm, three pieces. Dear god, were they going to the opera? Perhaps her mini wasn't appropriate. Kathryn felt that insecure, nervous feeling return. She automatically felt inadequate, like she wasn't pretty enough for this guy. In fact, Matthew seemed prettier than she was.

But, instead of focusing on the growing anxiety within her, Kathryn decided to put her attention on what was right in front of her. At that very moment it was Matthew. He came over, gave her a quick hug, and then jetted over to the bar to order. Relieved to have a minute to address her anxiety, Kathryn made her way to the bathroom to take a look. Was it true? Had she somehow transformed from the beautiful, confident woman she was when she left her apartment to an insecure, ugly girl? In the bathroom, her worst fears were true. Suddenly, all she could see was everything that was wrong with her appearance. Did he notice? Was that why he had been curt, only giving her a quick hug and then scurrying to the bar?

Kathryn realized she was being unnecessarily neurotic. And the only thing to do when one is being neurotic is to breathe. So, she locked herself in a stall and began taking big, deep breaths. Why did she feel so nervous and insecure on her dates with Matthew? If Matthew was The One, there was nothing to worry about. This thought calmed her nerves. She was putting entirely too much pressure on things and it was making it impossible for her to act like herself. She had to simmer down. Now. Another deep breath and she found herself feeling a little more relaxed. She was going to enjoy the evening. She deserved to soak in this experience.

Kathryn emerged from the bathroom with renewed confidence and walked (catwalk style—take that Tyra Banks!) to where Matthew was sitting, armed with what looked like a dirty martini. She sat kitty-corner from him on the couch and smiled.

"You have amazing legs, Kathryn." Matthew smiled up at her.

She secretly thanked the Universe for allaying her fears.

"You have on an incredibly detailed three-piece suit, Matthew," she teased.

He seemed serious. "I try to dress my best for every occasion."

"Oh, yeah, of course." Yikes, she needed to change the subject. But, that was done rather quickly all by itself.

At that very moment, two beautiful blondes walked into the bar, wearing what could only be described as spandex that covered so little there was nothing left to the imagination and too much for what a stripper might need for a successful night working. Kathryn, feeling both admiration (not an easy look to pull off) and concern (how would she feel about her potential soul mate staring at these women?) turned to Matthew to change the subject to something more appropriate. Only it was impossible for Matthew to even notice Kathryn—his eyes were glued to both women, and his mouth was wide open in what looked to be very much like a state of delight.

What. In the world. Was he doing.

Kathryn stared at him in disbelief. She was pretty sure that this was not how she wanted her soul mate to act. Was he 15? She kept her eyes on him, but he didn't seem to notice. Typically, if she was dating a man and he exhibited such outlandish behavior, she would call him on it, right then and there. She would actually walk out if it was any other man. But, this was quite potentially the love of her life. She had to find an appropriate way of handling the situation. Unfortunately, Kathryn had zero ideas as to what his need for such ridiculous behavior might be. Mid-thought, Matthew finally turned his attention from ogling the two women to her.

"Oh. Oops." He grinned boyishly. "Did you see that?"

"Which part? You ogling women right in front of me while we're on a date or the two blondes who were barely clothed?"

"Don't hate on them Kathryn. They're merely beautiful women showing the world their beauty."

Wait—was that her gag reflex kicking in? Kathryn wasn't entirely sure, but she *was* sure she could literally feel her blood boiling. She was about to have a serious reaction on Mr. Matthew if she wasn't careful.

"Perhaps we could focus on something more centered on our evening, and you and I. What do you think of that?"

She wasn't even sure where that calm response came from, but she was happy with it. She had found a way to let him know what she needed right then, without throwing her delicious (not to mention refreshing) vodka soda in his face, while then storming out. Besides, they *were* beautiful women, even she had noticed them.

"Why Kathryn, I think that is a perfect idea."

He smiled gently at her. She almost forgave him.

The rest of the evening passed uneventfully as Matthew somehow figured out how to control himself from blatantly checking out other women while on their date. They discussed a number of fascinating subjects—the new book Kathryn was working on (she had begun compiling all of her poetry together for a new book), the way to end world poverty (Kathryn was sure it was micro-credit lending while Matthew felt it would be a combination of that and a more socialized government), and David Deida.

Deida was not an author Kathryn was familiar with before meeting Matthew. But, after hearing about his affection for the author on their first date, she decided to do some research. In fact, she had spent an entire evening at Powell's Books reading the majority of Deida's *The Way of the Superior Man*. She agreed with some of it—particularly Deida's explanation around the use and needs of masculine and feminine energy, but found some of it a bit extreme, such as the admonition that men should not ejaculate (what fun was that?). In any event, it provided some rich and dramatic conversation, something Kathryn loved.

After a few hours, they were both growing tired.

"Why don't we walk over to my place? I can show you my stunning view of the Fremont Bridge and we can have a glass of wine. I think I've got a bar of Theo organic dark chocolate as well." He winked.

Theo was her fave chocolate—he had been paying attention. This made Kathryn very, very happy.

"Sure, that sounds lovely. And let me be clear—I'm most interested in seeing this view of the Fremont Bridge—I didn't know it was a 'thing.'" She smiled; the two vodka sodas were getting to her a bit.

Matthew seemed to be in the same place with his dirty martinis.

"You know, people pay me very good money to see my views of the Fremont Bridge." He winked again.

They walked arm and arm to his condo in the Pearl. Kathryn
was impressed that at 25, Matthew had purchased a condo in one
of Portland's trendiest and most expensive areas. She only rented
hers, although she often wondered if she should buy one. While he
punched in his security code, Kathryn set her chin on his shoulder.
He looked over at her and smiled. The anxiety was gone, she was
now feeling peaceful.

His condo was only on the third floor, but even so, Matthew insisted on taking the elevator. Kathryn was too tipsy to argue. As they
got into the elevator, Matthew leaned into her. He placed his hand
on her face. Oh, the hand-to-face move. She was defenseless against
it. Suddenly he pressed his lips on her, his tongue eager and intense
inside her mouth. Kathryn let out a slight moan as he pushed her
legs apart and picked her up—her legs now straddling his waist. He
could pick her up so easily, and she liked that. A man who could
move her around. He was going to come in handy, Kathryn thought.
She grabbed the back of his head, meeting his intensity with hers.
Her tongue danced with his. She was trying to find his rhythm, find
their rhythm, but it escaped her.

The elevator beeped. They were on his floor. He pulled away from
her quickly, grabbed her hand, and led her to his apartment. She hadn't
seen this kind of intensity coming, but she would take it. Her heart
continued to race as he opened the door and led her inside.

Matthew's apartment was immaculate. There didn't seem to be
a piece out of place, let alone dust on the floor. The white leather
couch was the centerpiece of the living space with a glass-top bamboo coffee table, a modern glass desk that housed a large flat screen
for his computer, a book case so tall it almost touched the ceiling—
and wait, were the books actually in alphabetical order? It appeared
they were. The kitchen and dining area were decorated in black and
white, with a glass dining table bringing the room together. It was
minimalist meets industrialist meets over-the-top modern.

Kathryn was shocked. First, that a man of 25 would keep a house cleaner than her own mother (who was known to be slightly OCD when it came to cleanliness, often resulting in 4 a.m. cleanings during Kathryn's childhood) and secondly, that her own home couldn't hold a candle to his. Who has the time to keep everything this clean? As she surveyed the apartment, she noticed a copy of *The Enlightened Sex Manual* by David Deida on Matthew's coffee table. She filed that away in her memory as well. Something for her to explore during her next jaunt to Powell's.

"You seem deep in thought. Pondering our little elevator escapade?" He handed her a glass of red.

"Hmm…yes. That was nice, and totally unexpected. You continue to surprise me Matthew."

"Well, that's what I'm going for."

If only he knew the real surprise—they were actually meant to spend their lives together! In Europe! Running sustainable farms! She wondered if he felt any hint of this. In everything she had read, soul mates feel a resonance with their other right away. She hoped he was tuning in to their connection. Matthew had turned on some Sade, one of Kathryn's favorite artists. He dimmed the lights and Kathryn felt a twinge—of something she wasn't sure of. It wasn't excitement and it wasn't repulsion, it was somewhere in the middle. Something was definitely up.

Matthew walked over to Kathryn, looking directly into her eyes. He grabbed her wine glass, set it on a coaster (of course) on the bamboo coffee table and pulled Kathryn to him. He kissed her, again, this time forcefully. Again, she couldn't find his or their rhythm. It was like he was trying to devour her face. With his mouth. And with the hotness of the elevator gone, she just couldn't get into it. Clearly feeling this, he pulled back and looked at her.

"Are you not ready?"

She looked down, unsure of what he was asking.

"Ready for what exactly?"

"Oh, never mind." Matthew pulled away, grabbed his wine glass and sat on the leather sofa, carefully crossing one leg over the other, an arm on the back of the couch.

"Oh, you mean ready for your stellar view of the Fremont Bridge? Well, yes, actually, I am ready for that. Let's open up those blinds."

Matthew didn't move, but Kathryn didn't falter. She walked over to the couch, and pulled the blinds back. She wasn't sure what he was doing or why he was pouting, but she wasn't going to let it ruin a perfectly wonderful evening. Besides, Matthew was right, the view was quite beautiful.

"Wow, Matthew, I thought you were messing with me, but you're right—this really is gorgeous."

The city lights surrounded the bridge, while the American flag at the top rippled perfectly in the soft breeze. Kathryn sighed, she truly loved this city.

"You know Kathryn, I'm quite tired and it's already after midnight. I think it's time to call it a night. I'm sure you're not walking home. So, are you taking the streetcar or shall I call you a cab?"

What? He was kicking her out? Because she wasn't throwing herself all over him on their second date? Her mind zigzagged throughout the details, Samorio's prophecy, Matthew's desire to be a sustainable farmer, their synchronistic meeting. Didn't he know who she was? Didn't he know what was happening?

She looked into his eyes, but saw there was nothing there. He was gone, staring over at her as if she was some annoyance that needed to be dealt with. Kathryn couldn't understand how things could unravel so quickly in one evening. She wanted to go to him, to hold him, and whisper in his ear—anything that would make him remember. That would remind him that they were meant to be, that love was the only way. At this point though, Kathryn's intuition told her it wouldn't work. Something had triggered him and it wasn't going to be resolved that night.

"Suit yourself Matthew. I have no clue what you're angry about, but if it's because I wasn't begging to sleep with you on our second date, then I don't have anything to say to you."

"Kathryn, this is more than our second date. We've spent time together with our friends on many, many occasions."

He was practically rolling his eyes at her. What nerve! And hanging out in a group without ever speaking did not count as previous time spent together. What was wrong with him? Tears filled her eyes. She could not understand his behavior. It was not supposed to be like this. He was not supposed to be like this. It was all supposed to be going differently. Couldn't he see her light? Didn't he remember?

"Goodnight Matthew."

Kathryn was afraid if she kept talking she would burst into tears and that was the last thing she wanted to do. Bypassing the elevators, she ran down the stairs, tears streaming down her face. She was confused and did not know what the Universe was doing. She felt like the victim of some cruel game, one where she finds her great love, only to be totally humiliated and rejected by him.

Standing outside waiting for the streetcar, the tears continued to fall, and by this time Kathryn didn't care if anyone noticed. She had met her One and he had proceeded to ogle other women right in front of her and kick her out of his place when she didn't respond the way he thought she should to his sexual advances. Kathryn could feel her faith in the Universe, Samorio, and Matthew slowly fading as she stood there crying. What was all of this about?

She sat on the streetcar with a tear-stained face and anger in her heart. She had worked so hard to call in her great love, and here he was before her, and he was a total douchebag.

Chapter 5

"For the warrior of light there is no such thing as an impossible love.
He is not intimidated by silence, indifference or rejection. He knows that,
behind the mask of ice that people wear, there beats a heart of fire.
Without love, he is nothing." –Paulo Coelho

Immediately upon waking, Kathryn knew she was in trouble. She could feel the beginnings of a low-grade depression settling in. Her head pounded as she replayed the night's events over in her mind. From there, her mind set out on the task of analyzing, reviewing, and comparing what had happened the night before at Matthew's apartment to the data the Universe had presented her with. First, she focused in on her initial date with Matthew, and on Samorio's words about him and the farm. How could she have been wrong? She did exactly as the Universe instructed by following the signs.

The only thing that would cure Kathryn now was an emergency meet-up with Jess. Jess was "The One" when it came to helping Kathryn find meaning out of no meaning, to soothe her fears that the Universe was surely out to get her, and to develop a game plan that made Kathryn feel more in control. Control, of course, was only an illusion; Kathryn knew this intellectually, but still physically and emotionally craved it. How was it she could manifest a wonderful man coming into her life, but could never seem to manifest a meaningful, soulful relationship? It was a complete conundrum for Kathryn. Here she was, the master of her domain in career and friends, and family, and yet sometimes, no matter what she did, life took her in another direction.

It was at moments like these that Kathryn's faith was most tested. It was moments like these when she threw herself into a state of total victimhood, as well as a few pints of Chocolate Hazelnut Fudge Coconut Bliss. Thank god she was set to leave for Brazil soon—after last night's date with Matthew, she could not wait to be as far from Portland as possible. She couldn't trust a psychic, nor could she trust a man who matched up to said psychic's prediction. Kathryn sighed, still lying in bed, with her pink heart robe wrapped around her, feeling sorry for herself. Hadn't she set her intentions, worked with various healers to clear and heal her wounds all the while staying open to whatever the Universe had in store for her?

It just didn't make any sense.

⟋⟍

"Well, it's clear to me," Jess said in between bites of hummus and lentil chips. "He's not The One."

Kathryn dusted her salty hands off as she reached for another chip. She paused to access her thoughts. But, she was having trouble not getting distracted—Washington Park was chock-full of people due to the exceptional July weather. Whenever the sun made an appearance in Oregon, people flocked to outdoor spaces. They also immediately donned shorts and bathing suits, whether or not it was entirely appropriate. Kathryn made a face, first at Jess's unwanted ruling of the situation and then at the man in a speedo who was busily setting down a blanket not far from where she and Jess were picnicking. She pointed him out to Jess, who screamed with laughter. She had to admit it was pretty ridiculous.

"Okay. I will not let the scary speedo get me off track. I hear what you're saying Jess, *but* Samorio said his name was Mathew and he would run sustainable farms in Europe, and that's exactly what this Matthew wants to do!"

"So...Samorio is wrong Kathryn. Psychics, even the holiest of holy, can get it wrong. Your soul mate would *not* kick you out of his apartment because you wouldn't have sex with him. That's just not right. The Universe isn't cruel. C'mon, you know this."

"I don't understand. I was so sure. Maybe I've done something wrong to create this. Perhaps I have some sexual block that is creating this. Even so, I am not ever having sex with anyone on a second date. That just isn't right for me, I don't care what a man says or whether he's The One or not," Kathryn put her hands to her head and slowly started massaging her temples.

Jess reached over and put her hand on Kathryn's knee.

"Look at me."

Kathryn tentatively looked up; unsure of what Jess would have her do next. When Kathryn had decided to write her first poetry book and self-publish, Jess made her jump up and down screaming with joy while in a restaurant to celebrate the success. While Jess truly embodied someone who lived in every moment and was determined to feel every second of bliss, Kathryn was often far more conservative. The last thing she wanted was to have Jess make her take part in some silly coaching exercise to "free herself" by taking off her shirt and running through Washington Park or something of that nature.

She attempted to focus in on Jess.

"This is not your fault. You did not do anything wrong. You listened, you followed, and you were led somewhere that you're now not comfortable with. That's okay. In fact, how do you know that Samorio didn't lead you to this guy so you could learn how to set boundaries?"

Hmm…that she didn't know. Perhaps there was some sense to be made out of all of the nonsense. Perhaps she was still on a truth-seeking journey even if it felt like she had dead-ended in asshole-ville. Matthew did have something to teach her and maybe focusing in on him being "The One" was totally killing her ability to see what it was.

As if reading her thoughts, Jess said, "So, are you going to call him to find out what more you need to learn?"

"No. He can call me. Universal fate or not, the dude kicked me out of his place because I wasn't game to have sex with him right away. My ego is going to take a stand on this one. He'll have to come to me."

With that, Jess high-fived her and the two dug into their picnic of marinated olives, feta cheese, cucumber slices, dates and chilled Montinore Estate Gewürztraminer. Kathryn could feel the edge of her depressive state lift. There had to be a reason for all of this, she just had to remain open to it. And if it was truly about setting boundaries, then her boundary was set. She would not have anything to do with a man who treated her that way—psychically appointed "The One" or not.

⌒

The best way for Kathryn to pull herself out of any sad state was three-fold: time with Jess (check), delicious treats for herself (wine and picnic in the park—check) and spiritual practice with other like minded individuals. With her trip to Brazil looming, she knew she had to find a way to feel connected amidst all of the chaos that inhabited her mind. So, when she saw a posting for a Kirtan that night via Facebook she jumped at the chance to attend.

Kirtan is call-and-response chanting often performed in India's devotional traditions. Or in the home of a kirtankar, as was the case for Kathryn. At this group, they chanted mantras to the accompaniment of instruments like the harmonium, drums, and symbols. She had never heard any of the chants before and often couldn't pronounce the words, but she loved how over time the chants sounded like music and she could sing them as they carried her off to a peaceful place.

Kirtan was one of those spiritual practices that allowed Kathryn to get out of her head and into her heart, something she needed. It was a low-maintenance event, so she put on a gray cotton, knee-length flowing skirt and a white tank top with sandals. She grabbed her pillow for sitting (the group sat on the hardwood floor of the kirtankar's living room) and jumped in her Prius. She was ready to escape the chatter of her mind.

As she climbed the steep flight of steps to the Kirtan, Kathryn's mind drifted to her current state of affairs. She wondered (rather furiously) how it would all play out, if Jess was right and Samorio was truly wrong—but someone quickly caught her eye, snapping her back to reality. Sitting on the deck, staring out at the gorgeous views of Mount Hood was Scott. He looked just as surprised to see her, but recovered more quickly than she. Kathryn's mouth was still open as she pointed at him and said, "Wh-what are you doing here?"

She couldn't believe it. Scott practiced Kirtan? Was the Universe turning upside down on her or what? She had no reason to believe he wouldn't practice, but it still caught her off guard. She knew very few men personally who enjoyed the same types of spiritual practices she did. They always seemed to be old (Kathryn had nothing against old men of course, but she wasn't about to date a 60-year-old), gay (and fabulous, but un-dateable) or married. Now, here was a good-looking man in his thirties who had no problem chanting the name of god over and over again. Kathryn was stunned.

"Well, it's nice to see you as well, Kathryn," Scott smiled slyly, and only then did she realize how rude she was being.

"I'm so sorry Scott—I'm just completely taken aback. Normally men like yourself don't attend these events, at least not the men I know."

He smiled.

"Men like me?"

"I'm digging myself a hole, aren't I? Well, let's see, how can I explain this?" Kathryn fidgeted a bit, moving her weight from one hip to the other. "Men who are attractive, intelligent, and in their thirties. How about that? Does that explain it?"

"Perfectly." At this point he was beaming at her.

He came over and gave her a hug, a hug that sent warmth and chills (all at the same time) up and down her body. It was filled with so much...what was it? It was something she wasn't entirely familiar with receiving. Whatever it was, her body was practically begging for it, as she felt the chills travel up and down her spine. As he pulled away, Kathryn knew immediately what it was and fear filled her from head to toe.

The hug was filled with...love.

She quickly excused herself under the pretense of getting settled in before the Kirtan began. She immediately saw some of her friends from the Sacred Circle dance group she attended and started chatting with them. She had spent the last couple of years attending ecstatic dance once a week. Kathryn loved being able to be in a ballroom with a group of people dancing their asses off and none of the hassles of dancing in a club. Over time, she had made a few friends who were also regulars.

She attempted to focus on the conversation about area farmers' markets, but she struggled to keep her thoughts off of Scott, who from what she could tell, remained seated outside on the deck, talking with a few other people and taking in the view. He was blowing to shreds her theories that good-looking men in their thirties were not spiritually connected. How dare he!

Soon, it was time for the chanting to begin, and Kathryn relaxed knowing she would be able to vacate her busy brain and enjoy the peaceful melodies that surrounded her. As everyone took their place, Scott came inside to sit down. His pillow just happened to be placed directly across from hers. They would be chanting directly facing each other. Kathryn felt a twinge of nervousness, what if she looked like an idiot sitting there with her eyes closed, barely able to pronounce the words in each chant? Wait, why did she care what she looked like to Scott? What was going on with her? A feeling of unease arrived in the pit of her stomach.

He smiled at her and she graciously smiled back. They were adults; this was not a big deal. Kathryn settled into herself and let the harmonium carry her away.

"Gam Gam Ganapataiye Namo Namaste."

"Namo Namaste, Namo Namaste."

Kathryn loved the way the chants carried her off to another world.

"Gam Gam Ganapataiye Namo Namaste."

"Namo Namaste, Namo Namaste."

She reached down to grab her water bottle, and as she did she glanced over at Scott. He was peacefully chanting, a bright smile on his face, his eyes closed, and his palms facing upward. She sighed. He was so handsome and captivating. Why did she keep ignoring this?

Oh. That's right. His name wasn't Matthew. But what if Samorio really was wrong? Then she would be open to date whomever she wanted. *But*, her mind fought back—Samorio was not wrong. He was a man of Spirit and he had never been wrong for Hillary and Paul. Focus, Kathryn, focus. She tried to remind herself that she came to Kirtan so she wouldn't think about all of this. And besides, who said Scott was even interested in her?

Fortunately, she was able to get back into the flow of chanting and enjoyed being effortlessly swept away to a peaceful place.

"Ganapti Om Jaya Ganapati Om."

"Ganapataiye. GanaPataiye."

At the end of the last chant, she opened her eyes and saw Scott looking at her. He wasn't smiling and neither was she. For some reason, she felt solid and powerful, so she kept her gaze fixed on him. He did the same. He had the most peaceful eyes Kathryn had ever looked into. She felt her heart chakra expand, yet still, she kept her gaze on him. She started to feel like looking away, but that was immediately replaced with a determination within that she was unfamiliar with. She held her eyes to his.

"And that's it for tonight folks. Thank you so much for sharing with us." The kirtankar was closing the Kirtan.

Kathryn instinctively moved her eyes to the front of the room.

"However, we are going to wrap things up a bit differently tonight," he said as he began handing out small scraps of paper and pencils to his left and right. "Tonight, everyone who wants to will write down on a piece of paper a message or knowing that came to them during the Kirtan. Then, the messages will be placed in this large bowl in front of me and will be passed around the room. Each person who wants to participate will choose a piece of paper to read—as long as it's not theirs—and read it out loud to the group."

Everyone bustled with excitement. Kathryn looked back over at Scott and he nodded at her and looked away. Kathryn took a huge breath. The intensity of their eye-gazing had rocked her. She wasn't even exactly sure where she was. She turned to the person next to her, a man with a long brown ponytail and a half-shirt on (classic Portland hippy) to get her paper and pencil.

Silence descended on the room as the energy shifted from excitement to introspection, each one wanting to capture the message they had received from chanting the name of god for two hours. Kathryn thought for a few seconds before her message came through. She wrote it down carefully, making sure it was easy for whoever pulled it to read: "Follow your bliss and the universe will open doors where there were only walls.—Joseph Campbell." It was her favorite quote of all time, one she tried to live by.

One-by-one participants began to pull a note and read the words to the group. Some were filled with personal adages, others quotes by great masters, such as Kathryn's Joseph Campbell quote, and still others were verses from the Bible, Koran, Torah, and the like.

When it was Scott's turn, Kathryn was shocked to see him nod and then say, "This is one of my favorite quotes of all time: 'Follow your bliss and the universe will open doors where there were only walls.' Joseph Campbell."

He had pulled her quote. Out of 20 people, it was her quote that had attached itself to his fingers. Kathryn only had a few seconds to ponder this. She didn't believe in coincidences and knew the Universe was giving her a sign. What exactly that sign meant was completely unknown to her. She would have to take this occurrence with her in meditation, and better yet to Brazil. In the meantime, she did her best to hone in on what the next person was about to say. The last thing she wanted to do was to miss any pearls of wisdom.

Finally, it was her turn. It wasn't the easiest to read, but she did her best:

> "A man will leave his father and mother and be united to his wife, and the two will become one flesh. So they are no longer two, but one. –Matthew 19:4."

Becoming one. By Matthew.

Kathryn looked around. Was someone messing with her or was this real? Of course, she knew this was real. This was the way the Universe worked, especially when you're off your path. This was the Universe's way of telling her that Matthew was still "The One" and the two of them must become one. She couldn't wait to leave the Kirtan so she could call Matthew. She had been given the green light—and she was not about to miss it. Matthew was her One, the entire world seemed to know that except for him. But, one way or the other she had to bring it to light for him. She was leaving for Brazil in the morning, but perhaps she could catch him before she left to have one final connection. Scott was a distant thought in her mind.

When the Kirtan ended, Kathryn quickly made her way to the kirtankar to thank him, said good-bye to her friends from dance, and bolted for the door. As she made her way through the hallway, Scott rounded the corner.

"Kathryn, it was so lovely to see you tonight. It's funny how we keep running into each other, isn't it? Perhaps it's a sign that we should spend some more time together."

Scott looked directly into her eyes. The intensity threw her off, as though she had forgotten about their earlier connection during the Kirtan. She turned her gaze down, nervously laughing.

"It *is* strange! It's so hard to know what the Universe is trying to say sometimes, I suppose."

"Hmm…I'm not so sure, it seems pretty clear to me."

Damn him. She wasn't going to get out of this. All she could think about was Matthew and here Scott was trying to ask her out… or something.

"Well, sure—send me an email and let's have tea or something. We can try to figure out why we keep bumping into each other like this. I am heading off tomorrow to Brazil for a couple of weeks, but let's connect when I'm back."

He seemed to sense her distraction and nodded, leaning in to give her another hug. Although her mind was elsewhere, his hug seemed to bring her back—at least for a second—to the present moment. He smelled freshly washed like soap, with a light splash of one of her favorite colognes—although she didn't have a favorite cologne. But, if she did, it would be whatever Scott Lawton wore.

Getting caught up in him like this made her hold on a bit longer than she normally would, but he didn't seem to mind.

She slowly pulled away, looking up at him. "Thank you," was all she could muster and even then, she didn't know what she was thanking him for, it just seemed like the right thing to say.

"You're welcome," he said as he touched her face lightly with the back of his hand.

That seemed to snap her out of it. Whatever hug spell Scott had put on her broke when he touched her face. She had to focus. It certainly was no time to get caught up in some energetic high from the Kirtan. Scott was attractive, dreamy even, but Kathryn wasn't put on the planet for dreamy. She was here to find her One. It was, after all, her Quest. The reason she hadn't found him yet was because she always seemed to get off track by delicious-smelling, charming men. Well, not this time.

Kathryn drew back, softly said good-bye, and made her way down the steps to her car.

∽

Kathryn felt an overwhelming sense of urgency to connect with Matthew as soon as she got into her car to head home from the Kirtan. She wasn't sure how she would start the conversation though. The last time they had seen one another, he had asked her to leave because she wasn't in the mood to take things further sexually. It was an absolute disgrace on his part. But even so, the Universe was giving her signs that were pulling her back to him. Samorio *was* right. It was Matthew. She kept getting signs that said, "Matthew, Matthew, Matthew."

How could it mean anything else? They would just have to work through his clearly misguided sexual prowess. That's all. And those tight pants. Geez. That was going to take some getting used to. She took a deep breath and decided that somehow she would know what to say when she heard his voice. He was The One—if he couldn't inspire good phone conversations, who could?

As she picked up her phone, she saw she had just missed his call. If she hadn't been talking to Scott and getting caught up in his good-smelling hug bubble, she would have caught it. Damn. And this is why it had taken her so long to meet her One. She always seemed to get off track, chasing some other bright and shiny man instead of listening to the Universe. Kathryn stopped the self-flogging long enough to feel into her heart: should she immediately call Matthew or listen to his voicemail first?

Being patient won out as she decided to take a few minutes to listen to what he had to say. Perhaps it was something that would help her know how to better approach the conversation.

"Um, Kathryn, this is, this is Matthew. I know you may not be incredibly eager to hear from me after what happened the other night, but I promise that if you call me back you'll be pleased with what I have to say. So, well, just call me back, okay? Okay. Goodnight. And this is Matthew...not sure if I said that. Okay, bye."

Matthew was clearly nervous and wanted to hear back from her. That made her feel good, but something about the tone of his voice didn't resonate with her. She brushed it aside, arguing with her heart that now was not the time to analyze every little thing. She really wanted to reconnect with Matthew to see how things felt between them. Especially before she went to Brazil tomorrow morning.

She considered waiting until she was home to call him back, but honestly, couldn't wait that long. She felt an eagerness she couldn't explain. She wanted things in place; she wanted to feel peaceful about the connection between them before she left for Brazil. So, sitting in her car outside of the Kirtan, she dialed his number.

Immediately she heard, *"Hi, this is Matthew, life coach extraordinaire. Unfortunately, I am currently unavailable. Please leave me a message and I'll get back to you as soon as possible. In the meantime, check out my website matthewjohnsonlifecoach.com."*

Beep.

Kathryn opened her mouth, but nothing came out. She paused, and then hung up the phone. There was a reason they were not connecting before her trip. She didn't know what it was, but something felt off.

Driving home, Kathryn's mind raced—Scott at Kirtan and the noticeable connection followed promptly by the Matthew sign and the phone call. What was that energy she felt with Scott? It was intense, and a little bit...what was it? Familiar. That's what it was. But, she had to focus. Matthew was The One—Samorio had given her the prophecy. They weren't connecting, but the Universe was still sending signs.

Kathryn took a deep breath. She would have to find a way to relax and let the Universe work its magic. Matthew was her guy, she knew it. There were far too many signs pointing in that direction. She had to remember that the Universe knew best. She and Matthew would work through whatever it was that was keeping them disconnected and get back to their destined lifelong commitment. She was sure of it.

Chapter 6

"Love is the key to understanding all the mysteries." –Paulo Coelho

It was 5 a.m. and Kathryn was already awake putting last-minute touches on her impending trip to Brazil. Ovida and her partner Ralph would be at her place soon to go to the airport. Kathryn checked her phone one last time only to see that there was still no word from Matthew. Before time ran out, Kathryn decided to send him a quick e-mail letting him know she was leaving the country and to see if he might be persuaded to give her some clue via e-mail about what he wanted to tell her. She would do her best to sound open and ready for whatever apology he might present. She struggled to write the e-mail, starting and stopping several drafts, before finally deleting it all and writing something short and sweet:

Hi Matthew,

Thanks so much for the voicemail last night. I tried calling you back, but wasn't able to get through. I'm certainly curious to hear what you might have to share—you said I would be pleased and I most definitely look forward to being pleased.

I'm heading to Brazil this morning to see John of God and will return in two weeks. I will have intermittent access to e-mail, so please feel free to e-mail me back.

-Kathryn

With that, Kathryn signed off her e-mail, powered down her phone (she wasn't about to pay international cell fees) and grabbed her bag packed for Brazil.

⌒

"Bem-vindo a Brasília, Welcome to Brasilia."

The airplane jerked and landed with a thud. Frightened, Kathryn reached out and grabbed the arm of the gentleman sitting next to her, snapping her head over at him looking for some reassurance. The last thing she needed right now was to have her life end on a random inner-Brazilian airline before the greatest healing journey of her life even began. Or at least that's what the John of God website and Ovida and Ralph implied was about to occur.

"Por favor, relaxe. Tudo vai ficar bem."

The startled stranger began speaking in Portuguese to Kathryn. From the tone of his voice, and through her powers of deduction, Kathryn knew he was asking her to "please relax." It seemed as though everything was going to be okay. Hopefully. Perhaps they just flew differently in Brazil; and landing smoothly wasn't their number one priority.

She looked up the aisle for Ovida and saw her turn around and give her a thumbs-up. Ovida knew how much Kathryn disliked flying and was probably checking in to make sure Kathryn hadn't launched into a full-on panic attack from the rough landing. What she didn't know was that Kathryn had already accosted the nice gentleman next to her for reassurance. Taking a deep breath and methodically taking four deep breaths in, holding for four seconds and then exhaling to the count of seven (a trick she learned in a stress management class a million years ago), Kathryn turned and smiled at the man next to her and thanked him many times over.

He offered her some cinnamon gum and smiled, nodding his head. She grabbed the gummy, foil wrapper instinctively. Perhaps chomping on it would soothe her nerves. She hadn't slept much during the past 15 hours of travel—what with her mind churning about Matthew, along with her futile attempts to sleep upright in an airline seat. She made a note to herself, stressing over The One and sleeping upright would never result in actual REM sleep.

Kathryn surmised that what she really needed to do was manifest enough money to fly first-class internationally, and then she'd have no problem at all—even with boy troubles. In any event, the flight had given Kathryn plenty of time to overanalyze The Quest and her Matthew saga. Would he write her back—ever? Would they resume their romance when she returned? It all remained unknown. And god, how she despised the unknown. She felt quite antsy about embarking on this spiritual journey considering that her mind was fully occupied with securing a relationship with the other half of her soul. Tsk, tsk.

But, plans had been made and Kathryn had to remind herself that everything in life happened for a reason. This was probably *the* ideal time for her to be on a healing journey. At the time of booking the trip, she was seeking a way to access her inner guidance on a deeper level, to quell her anxiety, and learn how to better trust herself and her decisions. She knew The Quest would never come to completion until she healed whatever it was within her that kept real, true love at a distance.

And in her heart of hearts, Kathryn had booked the trip with the hope that whatever healing transpired at John of God would clear her blocks so her One could waltz right in. Wouldn't that be divine? Well, a girl could dream. Kathryn had read countless websites before booking her trip to learn more about what to expect, in addition to the book *John of God: The Brazilian Healer Who's Touched the Lives of Millions* by Heather Cummings. As soon as she read it, she knew she had to visit the casa. Ovida had shared numerous healing stories with her and told her about the culture—enough to give Kathryn a sense that she was in for a deeply healing journey.

As Kathryn and Ovida stretched their legs from yet another flight, they prepared for the final leg of their trip. It was now time to jump in a Brasilia taxi for the hour-and-a-half ride to Abadiania where the John of God casa resided. Abadiania was a town with approximately 13,000 residents, compared to the 2 million that resided in Brasilia, where Kathryn and Ovida currently were. The casa was built on top of a huge energetic vortex and one of the largest quartz crystal deposits in the world. It's been said that quartz enhances the healing energy that John of God channels.

"Táxi, táxi, por favor, por aqui!" Ovida's shouts interrupted Kathryn's idle and tired mind chatter about what lay ahead of her.

Ovida walked over to a taxi to discuss the details of the trip from Brasilia to Abadiania with the driver, while Kathryn chose to stay put outside of the airport exit, surveying the scene. Brasilia didn't look much different than any city, really, although the smell of the air was deeper, thicker, almost tropical. The people buzzed around in the same way they did anywhere else, and Kathryn couldn't help but notice the beautiful women who—despite the 90-plus degree temps—were dressed in skinny jeans, stilettos, and wore their silky dark hair down to their waist. Her own cotton khakis and aqua tank paired with black Dansko sandals paled in comparison. She thought about how Matthew had ogled the two women at Olive or Twist and wondered what he would do if he saw all of these gorgeous Brazilian women.

It was with this thought that she noticed she was feeling unnecessarily heated. She felt the distinct urge to drop her bags, which now seemed to weigh more than a million pounds, and begin removing her clothes. A flush of hot air came over her face. She was definitely not feeling well. Something was wrong and she had barely been in Brazil for 10 minutes.

Ovida turned to Kathryn to let her know it was time to load up and noticed that something was awry.

"Your face has gone totally pale, are you okay?"

"I'm not sure actually. I was just standing here and suddenly I felt hot and heavy, like all I want to do is curl up and sleep." Kathryn decided to leave out the part about taking off all of her clothes. Besides, the words in her mouth felt thick, unfamiliar. Her voice even sounded strange to her, as if it belonged to someone else.

"Well, let's get you into the car. It won't be much longer now and soon you'll have a bed to sleep on." She placed the back of her hand on Kathryn's forehead and smiled.

"Wh-Why are you smiling?" Kathryn slurred.

"They're starting to work on you already, that's all. Just breathe, and let whatever this is flow through you."

She hadn't even been to the casa yet, hadn't even so much as stepped foot in Abadiania, but "they" were already working on her? "They" were the non-physical beings that John of God reportedly channeled to perform his healing work. But, Kathryn was sure that she had to be in John of God's presence to have energy healing performed. Didn't she?? The notion seemed impossible to her. Although from the look on Ovida's face, something was definitely going on.

Kathryn said a quick prayer and collapsed into the taxi.

⌒

"Kathryn, honey, we're here, wake up."

Ovida's soft voice broke into Kathryn's consciousness.

"I didn't even realize we left," she mumbled.

"Yep, the second you got into the taxi, you were dead to the world. We even stopped a couple of times to use the restroom and get food. I could see you were so deep in it that I didn't wake you. They'll have hot food for you at the pousada. Let's get checked in—you're going to love this place!"

Kathryn rubbed her eyes, stretched, and realized she felt far better than she had upon arriving in Brazil. It was now early evening and the air smelled like eucalyptus and honey. Kathryn smiled. She was in Brazil. On a journey to heal her soul. She could hardly believe it.

The hotel they were staying at was called Pousada Luz Divina, and it was more beautiful than Ovida had described. The white exterior with purple trim and lush garden foliage made it feel like a tropical oasis. A waterfall, hammock, and labyrinth all greeted Kathryn and Ovida as they entered the property. Kathryn felt the peace of the place envelop and soothe her. She instantly knew why she had been so tired and overcome with heat at the airport. Her soul finally had a chance to make itself known, because Kathryn was out of the crazy bubble she had been floating in. Her soul was exhausted. She could feel that being in Brazil would bring her great relief and relaxation.

Just then, a petite American woman with thick blonde hair and dark-rimmed glasses came out into the garden to greet them.

"Ovida!" she ran towards them both with outstretched arms.

"Caterina, so good to see you!" Ovida replied. The two hugged and stood smiling at one another like long-lost friends.

"It's been far too long—we are so glad to have you back. And who have you brought with you this time?" she said, looking over at Kathryn.

"This is Kathryn, and this is her first time at the casa, or in Brazil actually. The entities have already begun working on her—the minute she stepped off the plane she started having physical responses." Ovida grinned. "She's going to have quite the experience here. I can feel it already."

"Well of course they're already working on you," Caterina said as she took Kathryn by the arm. "You are going to see things you never believed possible. And you are going to meet people who will become your friends forever and your life will never be the same. Are you ready?"

Kathryn smiled. While Caterina's proposal seemed a bit grandiose, Kathryn knew it was time to get to know herself on an even deeper level. She wanted to trust herself, trust her intuition, and be able to come together with Matthew healed and totally open to experience life on a more intimate level. She had heard amazing stories of those who had traveled to Brazil before, healing cancer, paralysis, migraines, depression—you name it, he had healed it through a process called psychic surgery. While Kathryn wasn't totally sure what that was, she was about to find out—and according to Ovida and Caterina, the process may have already begun! There were also stories of people coming to the casa and finding their one true love, as well as those who visited and never returned home. And the way Ovida talked about the casa made it sound like paradise. By the looks of it, that's exactly where Kathryn was.

"I feel as ready as I'm ever going to feel. I want to go deeper. My life depends on it."

Caterina winked. "I wouldn't be surprised if the entities started working on you from the moment you booked your trip and certainly within days before your arrival. That's just how they roll. Now, let's get you to your room."

Kathryn was taken aback. She had booked the trip before she even received Samorio's prophecy. Were the entities in on this whole thing? And was that why she and Matthew weren't able to connect? Were the entities working on her before—without her even realizing it? She had only been in Brazil a few hours now and already her brain was being blown to smithereens. She couldn't imagine what was going to happen over the next 11 days.

Caterina opened the door to a humble little room with two twin beds, two nightstands, a large window, a small closet, lamp, and a tiny bathroom. It was clean and simple.

"I hope this works for both of you."

"Oh, it's perfect Caterina, thank you," Ovida said.

Kathryn set her bag on one of the beds and looked around. This was where she would undergo major transformation. Except for the pocketbook-sized shower (Kathryn wasn't sure how even one person fit in there), it would do just fine. Finally able to relax and feel somewhat settled, Kathryn noticed how completely famished she was. In fact, she was pretty sure her stomach was eating itself. She needed food stat.

Caterina, apparently reading her mind, immediately spoke up.

"Come on, Kathryn, let's get you a hot meal—you must be starving."

Kathryn smiled. The magic had begun.

〜

Wednesday morning arrived with much anticipation for Kathryn. It was casa day and that meant receiving her first psychic surgery. Psychic surgery was described to Kathryn as a process where a healer performs a "surgery" on one's physical, mental, emotional, or spiritual body without the use of any medical equipment or touch. Even so, recipients are healed from whatever "illness" plagues them - whether manifested in the physical or as was the case for Kathryn - in emotional form. Psychic surgery is most commonly found throughout the Philippines and Brazil, and has been recorded as occurring as early as the 1900s, although Brazilians will tell you it's been happening ever since the beginning of time in their culture.

For those seeking psychic surgery with John of God, there are several established protocol, which is why visitors are encouraged to attend with a guide. When Kathryn first learned about all of the rules, she immediately knew she would have to go with Ovida; there was no way she would be able to do it all on her own. Now that the day was here, she was even more grateful for Ovida's presence. She was all nerves, as no one in Brazil seemed to speak English (although luckily, there was a large group from New Zealand staying at the pousada, so she could understand some of the people around her!) and she was certain she wouldn't be able to find the casa from where they were located.

She had understood a few of the rules though. She was wearing her all white attire—white knee-length shorts, flip flops, a white V-neck short sleeve shirt and her hair was down with not an ounce of product in it (which meant it was larger than life; in fact, she was worried she might knock over a few trees with what she was now referring to as her "jungle hair"). However, it was all per the rules. John of God recommends women wear their hair down to help the energy flow more naturally. That coupled with the fact that Kathryn's usual hair products did nothing in the face of the Brazilian humidity meant she simply had to surrender to the gods. She reminded herself that she wasn't there to look good; she was there to connect with her divinity. At least that's the rationale she used upon looking in the mirror.

When she stepped outside to go to the dining hall for breakfast, she couldn't believe what she saw—and felt—for that matter. Everyone was going to see John of God that day, so the entire place was abuzz at 7 a.m. to make the 8:30 a.m. start. The energy was excitement and joy, in fact, it felt like a deep buzzing was emanating throughout her body. It was unsettling. She looked around to see if anyone else found the vibrating to be difficult to assimilate. Everyone laughed and smiled—seemingly unaware of the growing fear and vibration building inside of her.

She couldn't stay seated at the dining table, so she got up and went for a walk in the garden. She needed to settle her mind, and her stomach. She was so nervous she wasn't able to eat. What would happen? Ovida didn't tell her much about the surgery, as she wanted Kathryn to have the experience on her own, free from any expectations. For some reason, Kathryn felt terribly unnerved. She stood staring into the field, looking at the light blue sky, when suddenly she heard a voice behind her.

"Getting nervous, eh?"

She spun around to see an older Australian gentleman looking at her, his green eyes dancing in the morning glow.

"Well, um…"

Kathryn could barely get those two words out before she completely burst into tears right in front of the man. He reached out and handed her a handkerchief.

"Oh, I see that you most certainly are. Now, now, it will be okay."

"I'm so sorry. I don't know what's wrong with me. I was pretty excited to be here. Yesterday, I'm not sure if you saw me, but I had a wonderful time lying in the hammock reading. But from the moment I woke up this morning, I have felt absolutely terrified and full of nerves."

The man laughed.

"This must be your first time I take it?"

Kathryn nodded, wiping her tears away as quickly as she could. What was wrong with her?

"I'm Henry, what's your name?"

"I'm Kathryn, thanks so much for the hanky."

"I did see you yesterday, and you probably saw the rest of us and wondered why no one said anything to you, right?"

In fact, he was right. Yesterday Kathryn floated along in a peaceful trance, feeling wonderful. She was eager to connect with other folks to hear their stories and learn more about their John of God experiences. But, while many of the New Zealanders and Australians who were staying at the pousada were out in the gardens that day, no one said a word to her or Ovida. It seemed like they were in another universe—their eyes focused on far-off places, no smiles or laughter like what she saw this morning at the breakfast table. Only this time it was her turn, she was far-off and unable to connect.

"Yep. We were all processing. Soon, you'll be on the journey, too. Well, that's not entirely true—you're already on the journey. The entities start working on you as soon as you make the decision to come to the casa and then things heat up the closer you get to arriving in Brazil."

Kathryn stopped crying. So, it was true—the entities *did* begin working on folks right away. She had checked her booking date last night online, and she had made the reservation to come to Brazil one week before the fateful Matthew prophecy from Samorio.

"Really? They start working on you that quickly?"

"Absolutely. Once you make that decision and you know what you want to heal, the entities immediately get to it. And it's normal to feel this afraid. But you've got to ask yourself: do you want to stay the same person? Or are you ready to change dramatically?"

"I felt ready, but now, now I don't know. I just have no idea what to expect and it's freaking me out. And I have all of this stuff going on back home that needs to be resolved and I'm just feeling so unsure about all of it." She handed the handkerchief back to him.

"One of the greatest lessons you'll learn here is this: you're not in control. So, just stop trying and enjoy the ride. Leave what's back home, home. You're here for you right now." Henry winked and turned to head back to the pousada dining area, gesturing for Kathryn to follow. "And don't bother trying to figure out what that means dear one. Just follow us to the casa."

It seemed everyone at the pousada was intuitive, as Kathryn's mind was already spinning on the revelation that she was not in control. How could he say that? She absolutely had control over her life. Didn't she?

They returned to the dining area just in time—everyone was getting ready to walk over to the casa. Kathryn felt her anxiety increase sharply, and then Ovida came over and gave her a hug.

"You're going to be fine. I'm here, we're all here, you are being totally supported."

"Thank you." Kathryn said feebly.

With that, they walked out of the pousada's entrance and down the road to see the great healer, John of God.

⌒

Except, Kathryn didn't actually see John of God. Well, not for more than a few passing seconds anyway.

What she did see were massive amounts of people dressed in white at the casa, which was decorated in white and teal blue. Ovida helped her find the right area to sit in for first-time psychic surgery participants, while she and the others went in their respective lines to go before John of God.

"So, here's the game plan, Kathryn. Kathryn, do you hear me?"

Kathryn felt like she was on sensory overload. The energy at the pousada and in Abadiania in general was a higher vibration, but this was a whole other level. She felt the buzzing through her body even more now that she was at the casa.

"I'm sorry Ovida, my body is buzzing and I'm having trouble taking all of this in."

"Kathryn, look at me. I want you to take a deep breath, okay? In fact, I want you to take several deep breaths. You are not alone, everything is going to be okay. I will be waiting for you after you come out of surgery. From there, we'll go pick up your prescription for the blessed herbs and then I'll walk you back to the pousada for your 24-hour sequestering. Okay?"

"I really have to do nothing for 24 hours after the surgery?"

Kathryn knew she did, but the thought of spending 24 hours straight on that twin bed was less than appealing.

"Yes, and it's for your own good. You will have had an actual surgery—even though your physical body will look the same—and we have to treat your body as though it's recovering from that. You may decide to stay down longer, but the casa advises at least 24 hours. I'll bring you food and you'll be fine. But, let's take it one step at a time, okay dear?"

"You're right. I'm sorry for being so out of it. I'm feeling very overwhelmed, but also very grateful that you're here with me. Thank you so much for taking such good care of me."

Ovida hugged Kathryn, gave her a quick peck on the cheek, and hurried off to her line. Kathryn did as Ovida instructed, taking deep breaths and busying herself by watching the John of God video that played on one of the television screens above her. English captions described some of the many healings that had taken place at the casa. Around her, Kathryn recognized a variety of different languages—Portuguese, Irish, German, Spanish, French. It was like a huge melting pot of nations all coming together for one common cause: to heal their pain, whether it was physical, mental, or emotional. It was really beautiful, but also overwhelming. The higher energy vibration, the different dialects all around, and the scattered emotions coursing through her made the experience feel surreal, like her old life was far, far away. She remembered Henry's words. She needed to leave what was home, at home, even though a part of her wished she could check her e-mail to see if Matthew had responded.

Kathryn decided to go sit in the casa gardens for a few minutes to get a better handle on her emotions and get a broader view of the casa layout. When she stood up, she immediately felt woozy, like she might pass out. She steadied herself by grabbing on to the chair in front of her. The woman in the chair looked up and smiled.

"Feeling the energy, are you? It can be a little overwhelming at first. Just take it nice and easy. You've got probably 10 minutes before they call you for surgery, so go out to the gardens and get settled before coming back in."

Kathryn was totally blown away. Help kept popping up whenever she needed it! And how did that lady know she was a first-time surgery participant anyway?

"Thank you so much."

"No problem, I heard you and your friend talking earlier, so I wanted to keep an eye and ear out for you in case you needed any more assistance. I'm Gladys, feel free to grab me and ask anything else if you need to."

The people at the casa were incredible. It was as if everyone was an angel sent there to help her through this process. Miraculous, and yet totally bizarre. This was going to take a while to get used to. She slowly made her way through the crowd out to the gardens overlooking a vast canyon. The day was beginning and the warm glow of the sun combined with the lush greens and tropical feel of the landscape was breathtaking. It was exactly what Kathryn needed.

She sat down on one of the benches and closed her eyes. She sat like that for a few minutes, soaking in the soft sounds.

"You're going to be okay, you know."

Kathryn turned around to see a young man sitting behind her.

"I'm sorry, what?" She was completely taken by surprise; she hadn't even seen him sitting there when she first entered the garden view point.

"I said you're going to be okay. You looked pretty frightened when you walked out of the main area to the garden, so I wanted to reassure you."

"Oh, thank you so much. Everyone is so supportive and nice here."

And handsome, she thought. He couldn't have been older than 23, but he was a gorgeous Brazilian man (Kathryn was starting to recognize various accents.). He almost didn't make her think about Matthew. Almost.

"Yes, we're all here for the same thing, it really bonds people together. By the way, my name is Daniel, what's yours?"

"I'm Kathryn. I'm assuming this isn't your first time here, then. Any words of wisdom for me before I go into my first psychic surgery?"

"I live in Brasilia, not far from here, so I come quite often. It's been an incredible complement to my healing work and practice."

"Oh, what kind of healing work do you do?"

"It's a blend of intuitive, shamanic healing. I was healed of bladder cancer a few years ago from John of God, and from then on I've dedicated my life to helping others heal. I realized that my body was screaming at me to turn inward and to stop seeking anything external for validation. I then learned from my time at the casa how to connect with my authentic self, and utilize my own intuition to help myself and others."

Kathryn couldn't believe it—he looked like a kid and yet he was a healer and had even been healed of cancer. *And* he had learned how to tap into his own wisdom, rather than seeking what was outside of him. The very thing Kathryn hoped to accomplish from her time at the casa.

"I would love to learn more about your story, but I think I better get back before they take my group in for surgery. Will you be around the casa today?"

"Yes, and I'll be here on Friday, too."

"How will I know how to find you?"

"If it is divine will, we will meet again. Have no worries."

With that, he turned toward the building marked "crystal beds" and walked off. Kathryn watched him go. She wondered if she would ever see him again or if he was just another angel sent to reassure her.

〜

Before she knew it, Kathryn was being ushered into a very small room with white walls and approximately 20 people. The walk to the surgery room made her feel woozy again, and it increased as she walked through the area where John of God sat and where others held what was called "current." (Current, as Ovida had explained, is where individuals sit—with their palms facing up, eyes closed and their feet firmly planted on the floor—to support the channeling of the healing energy for those that come to the casa). She saw him briefly as she walked by, his eyes ablaze, energy pouring through every cell in his body. It was so intense to look at him Kathryn had to immediately look away. The energy was noticeably different than what Kathryn had experienced outside of the main healing area. She swallowed hard, her mouth was dry. She did her best to take deep belly breaths and remember all of the people that had been sent to her that morning to let her know everything was going to be okay.

She sat down as instructed. A small Brazilian woman came into the room and stood before the group. The door closed, and everyone faced her.

"Now, dear ones, I am going to give you instructions in preparation for your surgery. Please close your eyes and place your hands on the area of your body that you would like to be healed. If you would like the entities to choose where to give you healing, place your hand on your heart. Do not open your eyes until you are instructed to do so. It is very important that you keep your eyes closed during this entire process."

A younger gentleman proceeded to speak in Portuguese, no doubt reiterating the woman's words.

Kathryn liked the energy of the woman. She had kind eyes and a warming presence. Kathryn felt safer just by having the woman in the room with her.

"Please close your eyes at this time. Place your hand in the appropriate area and let's begin."

Kathryn did as she was instructed, and placed both her hands over her heart—if it was up to her, she would ask that everything that was wrong with her be healed in one session. She figured this way the entities could choose the best area to focus on for her healing.

"We're going to begin by giving you anesthetic; this will help with the surgery process and during the next 24 hours as you heal."

Kathryn smiled to herself. Anesthetic? They were playing this up like it was a real surgery or something. The woman then began to speak again, and this time her words came out fast.

"You are here to be happy dear ones, you are here to live your heart's greatest desire…"

Kathryn couldn't really hear the woman speak anymore; her voice had faded into what sounded like a distant tunnel. Soon, Kathryn realized that she was crying—much like what had happened in the gardens with Henry earlier that morning. She began to feel energy or something— she wasn't sure what—within her body move. Something was inside her right knee, tapping it. She felt movement in her pelvis, some slight stabbing pains, and a pain that shot through her chest. She sobbed more loudly. She couldn't control anything that was happening inside of her. The woman behind her was wailing, loud, painful sobs. Her chair was shaking as the man next to her jerked around so violently that his chair bumped into hers.

It was happening so fast that she couldn't make sense of it. Her mind could not catch up with what was unfolding. Just as quickly as it had retreated, the woman's voice came back into focus.

"And now breathe deeply dear ones, knowing that you are loved in every way…"

Kathryn realized she was no longer crying.

"Please open your eyes now."

Kathryn opened her eyes. Her mind was quiet. Her body felt tired. She rose as instructed, picked up her herbal "prescription" (participants are given blessed herbs to take as a way to keep the healing energy in their psyche) and filed out of the room and into the fresh air. Immediately, she saw Ovida waiting for her, a large smile on her face.

"How was it?"

"I-I don't know." It was all Kathryn could get out.

"It's okay, you need to rest. Remember you have to stay down for 24 hours straight. No reading, writing, computer—nothing. I'll take you to fill your prescription and then we'll get you to bed."

Kathryn smiled weakly and followed Ovida. She was far too drained to argue any further about whether she needed to stay put on a twin bed for 24 hours.

After the walk to pick up the herbal prescription and back to the pousada, Kathryn was surprised to discover that she felt re-energized.

"Ovida, I'm actually feeling really good right now. Could I lay out in the gardens or something instead of being cooped up in the room?"

Ovida handed her a glass of blessed water and some of the herbal caplets from her prescription. She sighed, "Kathryn, you have free will to do whatever you want, but I highly encourage you to follow the guidelines—they are in place for your highest healing."

Kathryn didn't always enjoy following "the rules," but the serious tone in Ovida's voice made her reconsider breaking this particular one.

"Okay, I'll try it. I mean, I'll do it. I can tell that you feel this is really important."

"It is. Now, I'll be back in a couple of hours to bring you the blessed soup and lunch. Okay?"

"Thanks, Ovida." Kathryn walked over and laid down on her small bed. She looked up and waved as Ovida closed the pousada room door, blowing Kathryn a kiss.

And so, Kathryn lay in a twin bed in a small pousada in the middle of Brazil, on a perfectly lovely day. She could hear birds chirping in the background, roosters doing their thing, and often caught the smells of lush flowers and the surrounding gardens filter in through her window. Unfortunately, none of that soothed her.

In fact, she felt downright antsy. She heard that some people slept the entire day after psychic surgery, and she had hoped that's what would happen for her. But instead, it was like her brain had been cranked up to 100 mph. Worries, thoughts and emotions coursed through her veins at a rapid pace.

Why hadn't she started her novel yet? What was holding her back?

Should she re-publish her poetry book as an audiobook?

Why hadn't she heard from Matthew? Oh! She wished she had thought to log in to the Internet before the 24-hour prison. Maybe he had written her back. Her mind imagined all the possibly grandiose ways he would apologize and resuscitate their love.

Why was Scott always popping into her life? What was the point of that? And that hug bubble? That was just wrong. He should wear a sign that warned people about it. It could make even the most grounded person fall in love.

Oh, and her hair. Audrey always told her to do something different with her hair. And right now it was huge. People may come to the casa and fall in love (this reportedly happens a lot due to the high vibrating nature of the casa energy), but that certainty was not an option with her hair the size of a small island. Ugh. Audrey would be disgusted with her hair and definitely chop it off if given the chance. And damn that girl—she had the best fashion sense. That was actually annoying. After all, Kathryn was the older sister—shouldn't she be good at things like that? Clearly not. Why hadn't the gods gifted her with reasonable-sized hair and a sexy sense of fashion?

On and on it went.

Even Kathryn was getting exhausted with herself after a couple of hours.

She attempted to take some control over the frenetic way her brain bounced around, by reviewing all of the people she loved and thanking each one of them silently for being in her life. She then mulled over the possible scenarios that could occur when she returned—would Matthew whisk her away? Maybe they could spend a weekend together on the coast.

But then, the craziness kicked in again.

Should she indulge her desire for a cat and get one when she returned home? She loved cats, but didn't want to be that crazy, single cat lady.

It seemed impossible to get her mind to settle down. It was as if the psychic surgery had lit a fire underneath it.

Thankfully, Ovida arrived at her door right on time with a tray of food. Kathryn had survived until lunch. Hooray! And even though she didn't feel that hungry, it didn't stop her from inhaling every morsel of food brought to her. First, she downed the blessed soup (which was chock full of veggies and beans, and had been dutifully prayed over by the casa volunteers), rice and beans, chicken, salad, and some peanut bars for dessert. She talked Ovida's ear off in the few minutes she was there.

Ovida watched her closely and said, "You may want to slow down, Kathryn."

"Oh sorry, I'm acting like I'm famished. I think it's because I'm so excited to have something to do."

"No, I don't mean with the food, I mean with your thoughts. You're going a million miles an hour. Take a breath. You're here to process, but also rest. You just had major surgery."

Kathryn giggled.

"I know, I know. It's like my mind got **über** amped up. It was so cute Ovida, right before the surgery, they said they were giving us anesthetic. Isn't that funny? Like they were really operating on us. No one even touched me. I felt a bunch of stuff moving around inside, but not one person did anything to me. What could I possibly need anesthetic for?"

Ovida looked worried and changed the subject.

"So, do you want anything more or are you all finished?"

Kathryn wiped her mouth and surveyed the damage. She had eaten enough for two people. Apparently psychic surgery made her ravenously hungry.

"No, I'm good. Thank you so much for visiting me and bringing my food. I'll do the same for you if you have surgery."

"Of course, dear. Now, get some rest. Why don't you try lying down and see if you can sleep?"

"You know, Ovida that's a really good idea. I'm actually starting to feel tired."

"I'll come back and check on you in a few hours, okay? Rest easy."

With that Ovida closed the door, leaving Kathryn by herself once again. Kathryn yawned, and before she knew it, sleep took hold of her.

⌒

With a sharp start, Kathryn's eyes popped open. It felt like she had been sleeping for days; the room was dark now and the pousada was deathly quiet. And even worse, something was terribly, terribly wrong. Her body didn't feel right. She turned her head to look at the clock. Only two hours had passed. She felt the need to use the bathroom, but when she went to roll over to get out of bed, she couldn't. She couldn't move. In fact, it felt as though the life had been completely drained out of her body. She didn't have a morsel of energy.

Kathryn began to panic. There were no phones and no way to call for help. And how could she explain what was wrong other than to scream, "Something's wrong!" It wasn't that her body hurt. She couldn't feel it—at all. She imagined that this was what people felt like before they died. Hollow, empty. Maybe she was hovering above her body and that's why she couldn't feel it. Whatever it was, it was bad. Tears welled up in her eyes and slid down her face.

What could she do? The pousada was silent, folks were out—at the blessed waterfalls, having crystal light bed treatments, or walking the casa grounds. Ovida said she would be back in a few hours. It had only been two, which meant Kathryn had at the very least another hour to wait. How could she do that? She could be dead by then. Her mind attempted to kick back into high gear and produce the worst possible scenario.

Kathryn didn't know what to do, but having a panic attack when she couldn't move a limb of her body did not feel like a good option. So, she did the only thing she could do right then: she began to pray.

"Dear Universe, God, Spirit: please, please, please don't let me die. I'm not ready yet. I have so much to do still. So much more I want to experience. And I have so much love to give, I'm on The Quest! Please! I promise I'll do a better job—I'll do anything you want. Just please don't let me die here in the middle of Brazil, alone, on a twin bed. I know I'm being dramatic, but honestly, I couldn't bear it. Please bring the energy and life back into my body. Please."

The thought of her obituary reading that she had died on a twin bed, was enough to produce a slight giggle inside of Kathryn. That was a tragedy she refused to participate in.

She wasn't ready to go—not like this. She didn't know who or what she had to bargain with or what she could offer up, all she knew is that she wanted to live the best life she could. She continued praying—thanking the Universe for all of the people in her life (this time with far more sincerity and depth than her initial stab at this when her brain was on fire), for all the special moments she had experienced, and for every wonderful thing that had ever come into her life.

And then, she stopped.

She heard something.

"You are so ridiculous!"

"I know, that's why I'm here—I'm asking John of God to heal my ridiculous-ness!"

Laughter ricocheted off the walls as the voices and conversation grew louder and louder. It sounded like a few of the girls from the New Zealand group who were staying at the pousada. They had exchanged pleasantries, but nothing more. For some reason, they were right outside of Kathryn and Ovida's room.

"So, we've got to talk American celebrities. Do you really think Brad Pitt and Angelina Jolie are in love or is it all for show?"

"Ohhh…that's a good one! But if we're going to tackle that one, we have to address all American celebrity couples in general. Are any of them real?"

The voices and laugher relieved Kathryn, and reminded her that life wasn't always heavy. Their presence also reminded Kathryn that she wasn't alone and she wasn't going to die. The Universe was hardly likely to have a conversation about Brad Pitt and Angelina Jolie be the last one she experienced! She didn't know what her body was doing, but whatever it was, she was going to be okay. She kept praying, this time thanking the Universe for easing her fears and taking care of her. Soon, she found herself in a mantra saying "thank you, thank you, thank you" again and again. The voices drifted on and Kathryn felt some relief.

She would get through this.

Two hours later, Ovida returned. One look at Kathryn and she knew something was wrong.

"What happened? What's going on?" she immediately asked.

Kathryn looked up at her pitifully. "I don't know, I slept for two hours and woke up and couldn't move. I've been laying here for a couple of hours praying and begging for you to come back. The ladies outside have been keeping me company, their voices and laughter really helped."

"I told them to quiet down, they didn't even know you were in the room. Oh wow, you look awful honey. Let me go see if that naturopathic doctor who is also a guide for the New Zealand group is here. We'll have him take a look at you."

She grabbed Kathryn's hand and squeezed it. "You're going to be okay, don't worry."

A few minutes later, Alexander, the naturopath and John of God tour guide from New Zealand, appeared. He checked Kathryn's pulse and felt her forehead. He looked down at her rather seriously before his face broke into a luminous smile.

"Your anesthesia wore off my darling, that's all."

Kathryn's jaw dropped open. The anesthetic. That was real? It was all too much to take.

"But, no one told me I was going to feel like this, that I would feel like I was dying."

"Well, everyone has a different experience here, so there's no way to know what your experience will be. And I've got to remind you that a part of you *did* die today. And now it's time to let the real you surface. My recommendation is to soak some rags in blessed water and put it on your forehead and abdomen. That will help with the healing process. Ovida, bring her meals, and don't let her get up unless it's to use the bathroom. Kathryn, you have to stay down and heal. Can you do that?"

"Since I have zero energy, I don't think that will be a problem," she said, mustering a feeble smile.

"You're going to be okay, kiddo. Just relax."

Kathryn rolled her eyes. Why did everyone keep telling her she was going to be okay?

∾

The next morning came without incident; the rags soaked in blessed water seemed to help Kathryn regain some of her strength. She was able to get up and hobble to the bathroom when she needed to, and then hobble back to bed. Her outlook felt better, too. Her mind no longer raced with possibilities and outcomes. For the first time in what seemed like forever, she was absolutely present to what was happening in the moment. And for the next two days, she slept for most of those moments. She came in and out of consciousness when Ovida brought her blessed soup and water to eat and drink, and to soak new rags for her. Her dreams were vivid and stunning.

The colors lit up like a sunrise on the ocean and she dreamed of all the people she loved in her life. There was no appearance of Matthew. In fact, Kathryn gave little thought to The Quest. Quite possibly for the first time in her life.

One night, she awoke at 3 a.m., sitting upright in her bed—everything was quiet and pitch black. It was a bit eerie, like no one else existed. But then, she began to see flickers of white lights above her. They came from several different corners of the room and hovered above her. She had the thought that she should be scared, but she wasn't.

She lay back down, and ever so gently went back to sleep.

The next morning when the rooster crowed (as it did every morning in Abadiania), she didn't feel irritated. She felt ready to rejoin the rest of the world.

It had been three days of isolation, but on the fourth day, Kathryn woke up with a renewed sense of purpose and an unknown emotion. She felt, for the first time in her life, peaceful. Ovida informed her that today would be her day to go to Revision—where individuals go before John of God to find out if they need another psychic surgery (Kathryn was praying that he would not require her to have any further surgeries), or if they were assigned to sit in "current" (channeling meditation). Kathryn spent the morning praying to be sent to current.

For the first time since her psychic surgery, Kathryn went to eat with the other Luz Divina guests in the main dining area, which was a lot like a covered carport with a protected cover overhead and open space on the two other sides. It felt as though you were sitting outside, even when the gentle rain fell on the lush greenery surrounding the pousada. The friendly voices and laugher helped ease Kathryn's John of God fears as she walked to the dining area. Immediately, she was greeted with smiles and words of affirmation. "There she is!" "We missed you!" "You look beautiful!"

And Henry with his toothy, gapped grin, "I knew you would make it through, love."

Kathryn scooped up fresh fruit and eggs, along with a small cup of green tea. Her appetite was starting to return, thankfully. She was sure that over the three days she had whittled down to virtually nothing. Fortunately the pousada room did not come equipped with a scale—but her sagging clothes were enough of an indication for her to know that she had lost some serious weight. Kathryn was eager to eat, and took her plate and sat down across from Callie, one of the New Zealand girls.

"The color is back in your face. That surgery gave you quite the start, didn't it?"

"It was something else, that's for sure. I was so freaked out and in so much pain. I had no idea that the John of God experience could be so painful. I imagined that this would be like a meditative retreat—all flowers and rainbows. But, it's actually been one of the scariest experiences of my life."

It felt good to be totally open with someone about her experience. She hadn't felt comfortable expressing her full fears to Ovida. She didn't want to seem like a baby. But, Callie was younger and Kathryn felt like she could share with her the raw truth of her experience. Callie leaned in, placing her hand on Kathryn's.

"It's different for everyone sweetie. Every surgery, every visit. You get what you need, though, I'll tell you that. There's a reason why your experience has been so intense. Perhaps to show you that this world is real? That there is something more for you to trust in?"

Kathryn thought carefully about Callie's words. In fact, they were still ringing in her head as she made the walk from the pousada to the casa. She certainly believed in the spirit world in a way she hadn't before coming to see John of God. She also had a newfound respect for how powerful psychic surgery was. Many people did have a meditative retreat experience, so what was she learning from all of the dramatic intensity?

Well, she learned that there was by far something greater happening in this world. So many times since coming to the casa, whenever she prayed or even thought something, the answer and person appeared. She learned that she was supported and being cared for, even in her most terrifying moments (and if being stranded on a twin bed in the middle of the Amazon wasn't terrifying, Kathryn didn't know what was). She also learned that when she got really quiet, she could hear answers to things that she didn't even know existed. Clear, crisp, clean answers. It was astonishing. Unfortunately, Kathryn learned that they were often answers she didn't necessarily want to hear.

One in particular that came slamming through the ethers while she lay in bed a couple of days ago was: "You are not in control." She had looked around to see if Henry was nearby. Wasn't that what he had told her? During another morning as she lay helplessly in bed, a slideshow of sorts popped into her head, cataloging all of her previous romantic relationships. It highlighted the lesson that each man had shown her and the purpose that each man had served. It was painstakingly accurate. She was also shown her role in each relationship; how her ego and wounding had impacted every relationship she ever had. It was in these moments, when she was too weak to think, that the truth slid into her reality.

It was after the slideshow that Kathryn returned her thoughts to The Quest, and more particularly Matthew. He had not appeared in that play-by-play, but someone else had. Someone she wished hadn't shown up—Scott. As she was shown their encounters, she witnessed that she was continually keeping her energy pulled away from him, never allowing him to see the real her or for her to experience the real him. From the second he outstretched his hand introducing himself as Scott, she had shut down a part of herself to him. This perplexed her, because it was the same thing she had done in previous relationships as soon as she saw something in the man that reminded her of something she had experienced before in relationship (that had not ended well). It was even more disturbing to Kathryn that Scott had appeared in the slideshow, but Matthew had not. But, she was far too weak to give it more than a momentary thought before sleep eventually overtook her.

Callie had been right in her assessment; having an intense, painful experience at the casa had forced Kathryn to have insights she would not have had in a more subdued environment. While Kathryn had come to Brazil to see John of God to learn how to "go within," what she had experienced was even greater. Not only did she realize how powerful and meaningful the spirit world was, she now knew with more certainty than ever before that she was not in control of everything that happened in her world. In fact, she would dare say she had far less control than she imagined.

As Kathryn approached the casa, her reflection on the conversation with Callie faded and something else came to the forefront— her nerves. What if John of God sent her to have another surgery? What if the surgery caused even more pain and she couldn't return to her life in Portland? Before the fears could launch into a full-on attack, a small, still voice inside said:

"Don't worry. What you have asked for is guaranteed. Go in peace."

Instantly, Kathryn felt a wave of chills that started at her crown and travelled down her back. Then, she felt a calm come over her. She knew intuitively that she was being protected; everything would be just fine. In fact, as Kathryn approached the various lines to see John of God, an attendant approached her right away and guided her to the correct area. She stood there as if in a dream state, not thinking, just being in the moment—listening to the tropical birds, smelling the aroma of the lush gardens, as well as the delicious scents of the blessed soup that was being prepared. When it was her turn to step before John of God, his eyes glazed over and focused on a far off place, and he said, "Está para ir sentar-se na atual entidade."

Via translation from one of the Portuguese guides, she was to go sit in entity current for the remainder of her time at the casa.

Kathryn felt joyful. She was going to be fine. She went and sat in entity current. This no doubt would be a breeze—sitting in current as opposed to being ill all by herself? Piece of cake. However, Kathryn should have known better. She was not in control, and life had plans for her that she didn't always understand.

And so, time passed.

And passed.

And passed.

While Kathryn couldn't be sure exactly how much time had passed, it felt like at least two hours or more. Unfortunately, there was no way to verify this information, because in current you cannot open your eyes and there is no announcement of time. She also had to sit with both feet flat on the ground with her arms and hands resting on her legs, palms facing up. It was hot and humid, and the large fans throughout the casa were no longer doing their job. Sweat trickled down Kathryn's face, back, underarms, and legs. How much longer could this go on?

She hadn't thought to ask others about the ramifications of current, she had simply assumed it would be a breeze compared to what she had been through. Her mind fought with itself pretty consistently. The monkey mind reemerged as Kathryn finally had time to "think" about The Quest and that slideshow she had been shown during her more lucid moments. No more downloading messages from the divine—somehow she had been transported back to true Kathryn, hamster-on-a-wheel mind style. She wondered about Matthew; what was he doing? Was he thinking of her? Images of Scott kept appearing—primarily images that had shown up during that bedtime slideshow—and while she occasionally gave them merit, she mostly batted them away. It was far easier for her to stick with the images she had created ever since Samorio had given her his prophecy and since she had met Matthew. She imagined their life in Europe working on a sustainable farm. She imagined their two little girls. And then thought how weird it would be to be pregnant and have a baby. Ugh. Maybe she would adopt. Even so, no matter how hard she tried to visualize this future, some part of it felt…off.

As soon as she tuned into that "off" feeling, she began to notice movement within her body—similar to what she experienced during her psychic surgery. Tapping in her legs again, now in her lower back, and over her heart, where it stayed for some time. There seemed to be a lot of work being done on her heart. Somehow she was able to relax into all of the internal energy work, and before she knew it, she heard the sound of thunder and felt a breeze skim her legs. A thunderstorm was coming to cool them off. The rain began to fall, and with that so did the temperature. Kathryn smiled. Once again, she (and everyone else) was being taken care of. Everyone was right—everything *was* going to be okay.

Soon after, she heard a Portuguese woman's voice announce that all of the healing had taken place for the day and that they were now dismissed from current. Kathryn opened her eyes and turned to find Ovida sitting right next to her. She smiled and gave her a big hug.

"That was one of the longest currents ever!" Ovida remarked, looking at her watch.

"Really? It was my first one! I thought I was going to pass out at one point—and then the thunderstorm came and made things so much better."

"Yes, that storm cooled us all down. I don't know how Joao (the Portuguese name for John of God) was handling it. But yes, we've been in here for four-and-a-half hours. I came in right after you."

"Oh my god! I essentially meditated for four-and-a-half hours?"

"Yep," Ovida said. "Welcome to the club, my dear."

Kathryn left the casa feeling more at ease than she had in a decade. She had done something she never imagined possible. She had sat in total silence, all the while channeling energy *and* receiving healing work from nonphysical entities for four-and-a-half hours. Before that, she had survived a painful psychic surgery. She felt like she had overcome huge fears and challenges in a short amount of time. Her life suddenly felt so wide and open, and free.

The rest of the guests at the casa must have felt the same way because everyone decided on the walk back (in what was now drizzle) to stop at Fruitti's café for tea and snacks. For the first time since arriving in Brazil, Kathryn was ready to socialize and do something other than process and heal. She ordered a ginger honey tea and sat down with Ovida and a few of the other guests from the Luz Divina pousada. Alexander, the naturopath was there. He came and sat down next to her to ask how she was feeling.

"So much better! The blessed water and rags helped tremendously, along with a lot of rest. Thank you so much for coming to check in on me that first day. I was scared out of my mind."

"Of course. I'm glad I was able to be there. And you did look utterly terrified. You look far more alive and at peace now. Although spending time at the casa will do that to you. What do you think the message was in having such a strong reaction to the surgery?"

"Everyone keeps asking me that and after today's four-and-a-half hours of current, I would have to say it was so I would understand and know that this is all real. If it had been a woo-woo meditative retreat, I would not have been as convinced of the truths I am learning from this experience."

Alexander smiled broadly.

"Well done. Can I ask—what did you come here to heal?"

"I came wanting to heal my connection to the Universe, God, Spirit, or whatever people want to call it. I wanted to feel connected and have access to a deeper knowing—something that I've always gone to psychics or intuitives for. I wanted to heal my second-guessing nature and learn how to trust the messages I'm sent."

"That's a very tall order and a very wise one. Do you feel like you've received what you desired? Will you go home feeling this was a success?"

Kathryn had to think about that for a minute.

"Hmm…I *do* feel more connected than ever before. I feel a deeper sense of trust. Now, it's about accessing my own inner knowing. There are still many things I do not have the answers to." Kathryn felt a particular stab of pain of still not knowing fully for herself who her "One" was. She had been following Samorio's prophecy, but that hadn't worked out so well. She hoped that as her healing unfolded she would get more clarity.

"Well, if you're interested, I have a suggestion for you."

"Yes, please!"

"Have Ovida take you to the waterfall. You'll need to ask permission from Joao. But once you have his okay, go to the waterfall and ask. Then, the fun begins and you get to watch what happens."

"Ask for what?"

"Ask for what you want." Alexander smiled again. Then he got up to leave. "It was lovely talking with you Kathryn. Happy journeys."

Kathryn sat in silence for several minutes wondering how soon she could go to the waterfall and what would be revealed when she asked her question.

∾

Ovida got permission the next day for she and Kathryn to visit the blessed waterfall. There were many rules to follow, just like at the casa. They each had to go into the waterfall separately as it was very important that the area was treated sacredly. There was no talking allowed on the hike down to the waterfall and once there, everyone had to keep their distance, so that each individual received plenty of private time under the waterfall.

Kathryn felt excitement building within her as she neared the waterfall. She knew what she would ask and she couldn't wait to see what unfolded when she did. A breeze picked up as she, Ovida, and two other women came upon the waterfall. The group was allowed to get close enough to view it, but then they had to return back to a place where it was out of sight, so each individual could go under the waterfall privately. The waterfall itself was breathtaking, although Kathryn was surprised to see the water coming down in a hard torrent. It seemed like it would hurt to put one's head underneath it.

Trust, she reminded herself. You are here to trust. There is nothing to fear.

She took a deep breath and asked her inner guidance (which she seemed to be accessing a lot more easily since her surgery) what she needed to know as she embarked on this interaction with the waterfall. She did this by moving her attention from her head (which contained less chatter than usual, but was still quite busy) and into her heart area. When she did this, she heard:

"Be gentle. Ask for that which you wish to know. And then let go."

Even though Kathryn didn't fully know what letting go meant, she felt peaceful by going within herself to ask the question. She was being protected and everything would work out for her highest good. She knew it with absolute certainty. While she waited for the others to have their waterfall experience, she came across a tree where several people had carved their names along with the date. Some couples had even carved in their initials like "B.C + H.K. 4-ever." Kathryn ran her fingers along the names and stopped when she came to a very familiar one. There in all caps was the name MATTHEW. Followed by the words "was here."

Kathryn closed her eyes, picturing Matthew back home in Portland. She smiled. He was with her, even from so far away. It would be exciting to share with him how he had been popping up in her life in such random ways since Samorio's first prophecy. It was so interesting how the Universe always seemed to be nudging Kathryn, letting her know—no matter what—this was the guy. Kathryn sighed at the thought; she didn't think she had ever felt so safe and secure.

Just then, Ovida returned from her time at the waterfall, signaling that it was time for Kathryn to go in. Kathryn took a deep breath, looked upwards and said a quick thank you before embarking on the path toward the waterfall. Once she got close to it, she couldn't believe how pristine and sparkling it was. In fact, it looked as though it were beckoning her to enter. Her initial worries about the force of the water vanished as she felt its peaceful and loving energy. She faced the waterfall and said, "How do I trust my inner guidance for every decision in my life?" As soon as the question left her mouth she felt chills—same as she had before—down her crown and back, all the way to her feet.

She took this as a sign to get into the water. She backed in and when the water hit her head and slid down her back, it took her breath away. Not only was it powerful, it was cold. Very, very cold. She let out a yelp. Automatically she felt afraid. The waterfall was a new experience and something about it triggered a fear response within her. Kathryn couldn't believe it—there was absolutely nothing to fear and yet for a second the coldness and force of the water frightened her. For a second, she was her fearful self. But then, she remembered. Fear was not who she really was. She began to laugh, realizing nothing could hurt her here; she was always being protected. The fear was simply a conditioned response within her that showed up anytime something new, different, or intensely physical appeared in her life experience.

Wait—that was it.

It was a conditioned response—nothing more, nothing less. Her fear—all of it—had been programmed inside of her from long ago. It was never real. Her fear that she would die from the surgery, was just that—a thought, a fear in her head. It was never real. The fear was not real. What was real was this—this bliss, this joy, this love. She needed her heart to remind her, and when it did, peace enveloped her. It was so simple: follow your bliss (Joseph Campbell had been right all along!).

The best way to access her intuition was to feel the quality of the response to any situation. If it was a fear response, she needed to ask, "Am I truly in danger?" If not, she could be sure it was a pre-conditioned response and not that of her higher self. Her higher self was bliss and would always respond in that way. Kathryn laughed, dunked under the waterfall one more time, and then skipped back to the area where the others waited for their turn with the magic waterfall. She thanked John of God as she walked back up the trail. At the top was Ovida.

"So, what did you think?"

"It was magic! I cannot believe it; the answer popped in right after I asked."

"That's how it works girl!"

And Ovida was right. Kathryn's realization at the waterfall was profound. She wanted to know how to work more closely with her inner guidance and the answer was so simple it was staring right at her. The answer to any question she ever had would be a loving, kind answer. If the answer was fear-based, it was not her intuition or higher self at work, it was merely a pre-conditioned response.

The evening at the waterfall marked the last full day and night that Kathryn would be in Brazil. She was overcome with much sadness at this thought. She had been able to stew in the magical healing energy for two weeks and she didn't feel ready to leave. That night, Kathryn had powerful dreams that seemed to be preparing her for the journey back home to face her Quest to find her "One."

Matthew was there, sparkling in his three-piece suit, while Kathryn was on the other side of what appeared to be a big ballroom. There were people everywhere and the design was quite futuristic. Matthew saw her, looked at her intently, and then looked away. Kathryn was waiting for him to come over to her, but he never did. She waited and waited, but he was busy talking with other people and seemed quite focused on the conversations. After a while, Kathryn felt pulled to move on; she couldn't keep waiting there hoping his eyes would meet hers. As she drifted down a corridor, she was instinctively pulled into another room where a man stood—his back facing her as he looked out into the night sky. She felt warmth spread throughout her body. There was something about this man that was familiar, and she felt excited to see him. As he started to turn around, Kathryn was jerked from the dream by the sound of a rooster outside her window, bringing her back to present reality.

Eyes now open, Kathryn turned to see if Ovida heard the rooster, but she had already left. Kathryn grabbed the clock and saw that it was 6:30 a.m. Ovida had a habit of going into the meditation room at the Luz Divina around 5:30 a.m. She should be returning shortly. Kathryn sighed, she could still feel this man's energy with her; it was so all-encompassing and exciting. She decided to let herself linger in that feeling for a few minutes longer—secretly hoping she would fall back to sleep and pick up where she had left off. She tried to hone in on the figure in her dream—who was he? And why had Matthew been so ambivalent? He had seen her, but had made no effort to come over to her.

Her inner wisdom was sending her a clear message, but it wasn't really one she could fully decipher just yet. With her brain in full functioning mode, Kathryn decided to get up, have an early breakfast with everyone one last time and say her silent good-byes to Luz Divina, the casa, and her first John of God experience.

And then, as if on cue, Ovida entered the room with two steaming cups of green tea and a big smile. Today, they would journey back to their "real" lives—if anything truly was real. After this experience, Kathryn wasn't so sure.

Chapter 7

"This sky where we live is no place to lose your wings
So love, love, love." -Hafiz

The return flights to Portland were not filled with as much anticipation as the journey to Brazil, but Kathryn did feel twinges of excitement at checking her phone and responding to the stack of e-mails that she had only been able to look over briefly on her trip (WiFi isn't nearly as reliable in a second-world country), as well as returning to her "reality." When she arrived home, she had a few missed calls from Matthew and one rather blah voicemail. He rambled on, clearly nervous, wishing her well on her journey and was "looking forward" to speaking with her upon her return.

But, it was okay, Kathryn's journey to Brazil had taken her both far and deep. She now knew how to access her intuition and would see what it told her when she saw Matthew next. She wasn't sure if her Quest was over, but she knew it was real. The insights at the casa had proven that to her. Her deeper feeling was—Matthew was The One. Just the name alone resonated throughout her body and it seemed to be everywhere; the Universe was continually sending her his name in signs. Besides, if his name carved on a tree outside a holy waterfall and dreams of him weren't enough to prove it, she didn't know what else could.

⌣

The days and weeks that followed Kathryn's return back to her "normal" life were not as eventful as she had expected. It was true, she needed to ease into her "integration" from the cosmic John of God bubble back to regular life, but she had hoped she would do a lot of that with Matthew. Instead, they had many missed calls, busy work schedules that never seemed to allow them to meet up, and a few meager e-mails where Matthew said he preferred to apologize and discuss things between them in person.

Kathryn had felt far more sensitive since returning home—the street noises seemed louder, she couldn't tolerate florescent lights, and found that she needed a lot more sleep than usual. It was as if her body was still healing. Ovida encouraged her to follow her body's signals and to take things super easily until she felt stronger and more ready to face the hectic day-to-day demands of Western life.

Finally, after what felt like an eternity (but was roughly three weeks), Kathryn was ready to come out of her healing zone and return to having some fun with her friends. Matthew and she had planned to meet up that weekend for a wine tasting that Jess had put together. But, at the last minute he had to cancel to meet with a frenzied client (apparently, his highest paying coaching client, making it all the more urgent). He said he would text her in case he was able to get out of it and could join mid-taste.

Kathryn didn't know much about wine (except what she liked and didn't like), but enjoyed the tastings just the same. Besides, she had been in healing mode for more than five weeks now; she was ready to have fun with Jess and some friends. She decided to go all out and put on one of her favorite dresses—purple strapless with a full skirt cinched at the waist and paired it with black wedge sandals—along with her favorite gold chain that had her initials delicately engraved on two charms. She swept her hair up in a messy side bun (she was attempting to channel her inner-Audrey with fabulous hair) and looked in the mirror, satisfied with what she saw. Maybe Matthew would stop whatever he was doing to stare dropped-jaw at her if he saw her. She couldn't help but smile. Her psychic surgery seemed to have shifted her self-perception as well. She loved being able to look in the mirror with appreciation for herself!

On her way out, Kathryn quickly checked her phone and e-mail for the final time—just in case Matthew was able to reconsider. But no, not a word from him. She sighed, looking up to the heavens with her hands outstretched in irritation, and then she smiled. She was not in control. She was going to have to tattoo that on her body as a reminder if she wasn't careful. So, she grabbed her white eyelet sweater and jetted out, ready for a distraction from her healing process, The Quest, and the constant missed connections with Matthew. Thank god she could count on good Oregon wine and her friends to distract her from the whole thing.

She pulled into the Wal-Mart parking lot at 11 a.m. in McMinnville as planned to meet the wine tour limo. Jess, Audrey, Jess's friend Cynthia, and her sister Brenna were already in the limo and ready to go when Kathryn squeezed in. No sooner did she sit down and get settled when Jess brought up Matthew.

"Have you heard from Matthew? Or are you following my advice and staying as far away from him as possible?"

"Jess, really. We have tried to get together, I actually invited him to come with me today (Jess looked as though her eyes might pop out of her head at the mention of this.), but we can't seem to connect. Our schedules and life demands are taking us in different directions. You know, like I told you, I'm committed to seeing him at least once more to see how things feel since all of the healing work I did in Brazil."

"Yeah, you're hanging on a bit more than I would Kathryn. The guy sucks. No one gets to treat my friend this way. Stay. Away. From. Him." The look in her eyes was actually a bit scary. "And besides Kathryn, why do you think you two have been missing each other for weeks? I mean, who does that even happen to? The Universe clearly does not want you two together. Take the hint already!"

Her sister Audrey—a big supporter—was a bit gentler.

"Maybe there is some deeper wounding that you're both meant to help one another heal. Perhaps you're just the person to help him with whatever would cause him to act so ridiculous." Audrey offered a weak smile. She wanted to support her sister, but the evidence against Matthew was beginning to mount and even the waterfall tree carving, dreams, and sign stories no longer held weight with the people in her life.

Those who knew Matthew were totally dumbfounded. Cynthia, who was closer friends with Jess, was completely flabbergasted by his behavior.

"Matthew has always been a great guy. I don't know what would possess him to act this way. Especially if he is your "One." It seems like you both trigger each other a lot. And I have read that soul mates often do that."

"Yes, Cynthia, I've heard that too. I am getting discouraged. It's not looking good for him, but Samorio's prophecy still rings in my ears. I have to trust the process."

"Process-schomess," said Jess. "Just be done with him already. And why don't you use your intuition to hone in on a better guy?"

Kathryn smiled, raising her voice, "Excuse me driver, we need to get this woman some wine—ASAP."

The girls started laughing and applauding—it was time to hit Oregon wine country.

Just then, the driver popped in, breaking up the Matthew debate.

"Hey ladies, sorry for the delay. Your group got placed with another smaller group and we're waiting for them right now. I got a call from one of the gentlemen and they'll be here in about five minutes. In the meantime, here's some water and snacks while you wait."

"Hydration!" Audrey shouted.

Kathryn smiled sympathetically at the driver. It must be a hassle to deliver that message to a bunch of girls who were ready for some serious wine drinking.

In any event, she was grateful for the shift in the conversation. How did she ever think she would get a break from The Quest on a wine tour with her friends who knew of her entire obsession with it? It was almost worse than being trapped in her head—especially when Jess got involved.

While the ladies waited, the talk turned from men to inner work. Kathryn had been very conscious of the friends she chose to have in her life, making sure she attracted friends who were on their path, asking the big questions in life, and open to growing themselves. She had given the play-by-play of her John of God journey via her blog, Facebook, and Twitter, as well as countless phone calls and coffee sessions to fill everyone in. Now, it was time to see what the other girls were up to.

Jess was working on increasing her meditation from 11 minutes to 22 minutes, quite unsuccessfully she noted, but she was hopeful. Audrey was just starting to play with the Law of Attraction and had already manifested a date, a free cup of coffee, and five new clients. Cynthia was trying out past life regressions as a way to gain more clarity about what she would be facing in this life, and Brenna, Cynthia's sister, was pursuing her draw to labyrinths and had already attended two labyrinth walks in the city alone. She hoped one day to build one in her backyard and hold events there. She had already grilled Kathryn about the labyrinth at Luz Divina and had made Kathryn promise to take her the next time she visited Brazil.

The conversation had gone from heavy (bashing people usually lowers the vibration anywhere) to inspired, as each woman shared her individual journey, where it was leading her, and the lessons she was learning. Kathryn finally felt relaxed, as thoughts of Matthew and The Quest slowly turned to great appreciation for her friends and for all the opportunities they each had to uncover their true purpose in life.

Finally, they heard a car pull up. All of the girls cheered, as the driver announced that the other group had arrived and they would be taking off in minutes to their first winery.

"Willamette Valley wineries, here we come!" said Jess, as they all toasted with their water bottles.

Unfortunately, that water didn't stay down long. Kathryn just about spit hers out when none other than Scott entered the limo.

"Scott!"

"Well, Kathryn, what a nice surprise."

Jess was immediately on the case.

"Scott, are you stalking Kathryn? You know, you can just ask her out," Jess teased.

Scott chuckled as he took a seat across from Kathryn.

"I've tried, let me assure you Jess, but Kathryn, as you know, has been a little distracted lately."

Kathryn immediately felt defensive, but wasn't about to let it show. Distracted? Yeah, well he might be distracted too if he was busy tracking down the love of his life *and* healing himself in the deep Amazon. She decided to keep quiet and let him have his fun. Frankly, she was so shocked to see him yet again that she could do little more than grin, as if she were in on the Universe's big joke.

Audrey shot her a look like, "How come I don't know about this guy?"

Three more people entered the limo, two other men and one woman.

"Kathryn, Jess, and ladies I do not yet know, please meet my sister Tina, her husband Dan, and my good friend Troy."

Everyone began shaking hands and exchanging names and information, while Kathryn stared at Scott. He smiled and stared back briefly, winking at her before turning to introduce himself to Audrey.

There was definitely something going on. She flashed back to the time on twin bed island (as she was now referring to it) when Scott showed up as one of the romantic relationships in her life. She shuddered internally as she thought about how closed off she had been every time she had seen him. Surely he could feel that energy from her. How embarrassing. She wondered, briefly, if he ever thought about her and why she was so closed off around him.

His presence in her life was beginning to be so obvious that Kathryn couldn't deny it. The café, the Kirtan, the wine tasting, her internal Brazil slideshow—this guy was everywhere. And every single time she fought it. She had been distracted, he was right. She was focused, yet again on her Quest, which by the way wasn't leading her to much of anything. Maybe, just maybe, it was time to abandon it— at least for one day. Maybe it was time to have fun, to enjoy whatever was in front of her, and stop trying so damn hard to make it be what she thought it should be. He clearly had some kind of message for her, at the very least. There was no way these synchronicities were meaningless. And Kathryn couldn't deny it any longer.

With that, she called out to Audrey, "Hey Aud, trade me places, I want to spend some undistracted time with Scott."

Audrey was up out of her seat before the words were even fully out of Kathryn's mouth.

Scott laughed and Kathryn sat down right next to him. He gently put his hand on her leg and said, "I'm glad to see that you've finally come around. I didn't know if I would ever see you again after I heard you journeyed to John of God. I had quite the life-changing experience when I went, and it was tempting not to come back."

"You saw John of God?" Kathryn's eyes widened.

"Yes, Kathryn I did. You seem surprised. Again. Every time you see me or we have a conversation and I share something with you, you're shocked."

"I'm so sorry Scott. It's just that, well, um, you aren't who I thought you would be—that's all."

"Well, I hope that by not being who you thought, you mean I'm more exceptional and attractive to you than you imagined I ever could be."

He winked.

And with that they were off. The limo driver announced that they would be at their first destination, Duck Pond Winery, in approximately 15 minutes.

While the rest of the limo chatted about the exotic wineries they had visited around the world (there was even a non-profit, Buddhist-based winery in the Willamette Valley, Bodihichitta), Scott and Kathryn were focused elsewhere. Rather than join in on the conversation, they simply sat next to one another and smiled. Kathryn felt as though they were sharing some great secret, one even she didn't know cognitively, but could feel throughout her entire body. It was as if the message was on the tip of her tongue. She felt slightly uncomfortable with all the gazing and smiling, but more at ease than she would have expected. She was incredibly curious, too. Who was this man, anyway?

As if reading her thoughts, Scott said, "You're probably wondering what all of this is about, eh?"

"I'm literally on the edge of my seat. Care to tell?"

"Well, if I were a betting man, I would say we have a soul connection of some sort. Hence, the synchronicities and continual eye contact without words. It's like we're communicating, but not in any language we know on a conscious level."

"Hmm…good use of data to draw a conclusion. I'm going to bet with you on that one. There's simply no other way to explain it. I bet we had a past life or two together with all of this nonsense."

"Most definitely. I find whenever I have multiple synchronicities with someone, there's some type of message there and well, I'll leave it at that."

"What is it? Do you know something more?"

Just then, the driver announced that they had arrived at their first winery. Although Kathryn wanted to know more about what Scott was insinuating, some part of her also felt like he would tell her when the time was right, and clearly that wasn't right now. So, in the meantime, she intended to enjoy herself to the fullest, taking in the sights, the wine, and Scott's company. For some reason, she had this knowing that she was about to learn something very important merely by being near him.

The afternoon passed in a way that moments in life that are full of total joy do—quickly. One minute they were sipping a light, dry Riesling at Duck Pond, the next they were taking photos on the veranda of Amity Vineyards, and then once again in the limo on the way to Mia Sonatina Cellars. Throughout the day, Kathryn and Scott always seemed to glide right along together and whenever they separated, one of them would come back around to the other. It was as if there was a magnetic pull, calling them to one another.

The vintner at Mia Sonatina entertained the group with fascinating stories about Italy, harvesting grapes, and why he left the corporate world to begin his dream as a winemaker. Kathryn was captivated by the man's passion and his dedication to creating the life he longed for. He was doing it all with his wife alongside him. Kathryn sighed. She always dreamed of that—of being with her soul mate and co-creating a life together, truly integrated and whole.

Out of the corner of her eye, she saw Scott looking her way. She turned to face him and raised her glass, he raised his and they drank. Somehow, she knew they were toasting some opening in their relationship—or whatever it was that was developing between them. Scott nodded for the door and instinctively Kathryn followed.

As she opened the door to step outside, Scott caught her by the arm.

"Come here, I want to show you something."

"Have you been here before?"

"No, but I still want to show you something."

Kathryn giggled, as he grinned from ear to ear, all the while looking straight ahead.

"Well, aren't you a mystery man. Surprise, surprise. I don't know if I'll ever get used to all of these surprises."

"Whatever it takes to spend some time with you, Kathryn," he turned and looked directly into her eyes. She felt her face flush, but she couldn't break away from his gaze.

She stopped walking. So did he. They stood facing one another and suddenly Kathryn's breath was heavy, and she noticed that Scott also seemed out of breath. He grabbed her hands.

Kathryn looked up as she felt tiny raindrops hitting her forehead. She looked back at him.

"Oh no, it's raining. We'll have to go back."

"We don't have to do anything," he said, rather seriously.

"I don't want to get soaked."

She turned away from him to walk toward the winery. Scott called after her.

"What, are you afraid I'll see your hair messy and your clothes wet, and I will think differently of you?"

She stopped in her tracks. The way the rain annihilated her hair had definitely crossed her mind as a potential hazard in this situation. She didn't want him to see her looking like that. Not when she was finally warming up to him.

"I don't care about any of that Kathryn. I only care about being near you."

And that was it. Hair or no hair, she would be damned if she let a comment as sexy as that pass her by.

She walked back toward him, and when that didn't seem fast enough, she sprinted in his direction (and Kathryn was most definitely *not* a sprinter) and jumped into his arms. His lips met hers as though they had been waiting an eternity to meet again. Kathryn wrapped her legs around his body, while the rain drizzled on them, wetting their hair, their skin, their lips. Scott's hands gripped Kathryn's ass and thighs, holding her firmly against him, pressing her flesh into his. His tongue danced inside her mouth, wet and hot with longing,

It was as if they had both been in a drought and the other had all the water they desperately needed. Kathryn could not get enough of him, her hands digging into his shoulders and the back of his neck, as though pleading for his body to press ever more firmly against hers. He slowly began to move, walking carefully in a direction Kathryn did not know or care about. All she could think of was him, having him, being near him, and feeling every inch of him.

He pulled away for a minute to lay her gently on top of a nearby car. She laughed. He pulled her legs apart and leaned in between them. This time his kisses were even more intense. Kathryn felt him pressed into her so firmly that she could feel his hardness. She arched her pelvis into him—her body craving him more than she could have imagined. He grabbed her ass with his hands with such urgency, she knew he was feeling the same way. It was magnetic, as if they could not control their desire for one another.

Suddenly, they were interrupted by laughter somewhere nearby. Scott carefully pushed himself up, panting, and said, "I hate to say this, but I think it might be time to head back to the limo."

"I'm afraid that you are correct."

They both burst into laughter. The sight of them must have been either tantalizing or absolutely absurd to any innocent bystanders. They were both wet with rain, Kathryn's sundress was hiked up to her thighs and their bodies were stuck together. As they peeled themselves off one another and the car, they saw where the laughter was coming from. Two couples were walking by with huge smiles across their faces, nodding in approval at Scott and Kathryn. One of the gentlemen even gave Scott a thumbs-up.

"Oh good lord," Kathryn muttered, rolling her eyes and laughing at the same time.

Scott leaned in and kissed her quickly on the mouth. "Clearly nothing they haven't seen before dear. Now, let's head back before the others get suspicious." With that, he swatted her ass and she galloped, giggling like a schoolgirl.

〜

After a long nap (wine tasting had a way of rendering Kathryn completely comatose, so a nap was most definitely in order), she awoke replaying the day's events. Had it really happened? Was Scott actually as deep, incredible, and sexy as she experienced? How come it took her so long to notice? And where the f*** was Matthew in all of this? Her mind churned on, until she no longer found it useful to lie on her plush sofa. She got up to make a pot of tea, taking some deep breaths to get back into her body, back into her soul, where all the answers awaited her.

With the water on to boil, Kathryn walked slowly throughout her home attempting to feel into her heart, while her mind screamed at her.

MATTHEW IS THE ONE, WHAT ARE YOU DOING WITH SCOTT?

WHY DID BEING WITH SCOTT FEEL SO MAGICAL?

WHAT IS HAPPENING?

MUST I DISREGARD EVERYTHING SAMORIO HAS EVER TOLD ME?

AM I AN IDIOT FOLLOWING SOME AFRICAN PSYCHIC WHO DOESN'T EVEN KNOW WHAT HE'S TALKING ABOUT?!!!

Kathryn's mind almost exclusively spoke in all caps—it was if she could see the words simultaneously as they screeched through her brain.

It was a friggin' battlefield in her mind; and it was clear that it would be of no real use to her in this situation. She had to get into her heart. In moments like these, Kathryn panicked. Meditating was out of the question, as sitting still seemed to further provoke her monkey mind as it thrashed about with its judgments, insults, and punishing ways. She would have to find another way to connect.

It was then that she remembered to dance. Getting lost in the music, allowing her body to move in whatever way it desired was a surefire way to let her mind go and allow her true self, her soul in. She opened up iTunes on her laptop, plugged in the speakers, and chose one of her favorite dance tracks, *Dog Days are Over* by Florence & The Machine. As she let the Universe guide her playlist (that's how she always viewed choosing the random repeat selection), she slowly released the chatter and the angst. She shook, yelled, and swung her head and arms as though she was a crazy woman at a rave—which she sort of was, minus the rave. She stomped her feet, but most of all, she felt. And in the quiet between Adele's *Rollin in the Deep* and One Republic's *Good Life*, she heard it. It was soft and quiet, and in moments like these when her mind had completely unleashed itself, her soul was a whisper. It said, ever so quietly, "This is The One."

Immediately her mind jumped in with, "Who?" Matthew? Scott? Someone I haven't met yet? But luckily, One Republic sang on and her body moved to the rhythm, determined to stamp out the power of the mind.

"Sometimes there's bullshit that don't work now
We are god of stories but please tell me-e-e-e
What there is to complain about"

She felt what she had hoped to feel in this dance—she felt free. None of it mattered. Maybe it was Matthew and Samorio had been right all along, or maybe it was Scott, or maybe it was none of them, but it didn't matter. She had a good life and really, what could she honestly complain about?

As the song came to an end, Kathryn couldn't help but notice that she was smiling. Mission accomplished—her vibration had shifted. Just then, she heard a knock at the door. She wasn't expecting anyone…

She quickly smoothed her hair, and made sure she was nearly dressed, her purple cotton shorts and white tank didn't cover much, but would have to do for whomever was behind the door.

When she opened it, she was shocked to see Scott. Holding a gorgeous bouquet of purple and white flowers.

"I was thinking about you and figured I should just come over," he said.

Kathryn couldn't help but smile.

"It's sort of ballsy dropping in like this. What if I had a gentleman caller or was in the midst of a crisis with my best friend?"

"Well, Jess is the one that told me to go for it, so I knew one of the items on your list wasn't going to be an issue. Besides, where do you think I got your address? That best friend of yours is pretty damn helpful when she wants to be."

Secretly, Kathryn loved surprises. What guy would go to all this trouble? A guy she wanted around, that's for sure. The two of them stood there, looking at one another. Suddenly, Scott broke the silence.

"Um, is it alright if I come in?"

"Oh, sorry, of course."

She stepped aside, letting him walk into her condo.

"And these," he said as he bowed slightly, "are for you."

She bowed in response.

"Why, thank you, they're beautiful. But you know before this goes any further, we've got to talk. Calling my best friend—what kind of sneaky move is that? Wait, are you trying to steal her from me? Because I'm not letting go of her without a fight," Kathryn teased.

Something about their connection made Kathryn feel silly, and so, she found that her sense of humor tumbled out whenever Scott was around. She loved that he could take it and enjoyed the teasing, too. He brought out a side of her she hadn't experienced since, well, since she was at least 16. Who teases boys anymore? Apparently, Kathryn did.

They sat down on her comfy cream couch, looking at one another.

"Kathryn…I…have to tell you something."

Oh boy. They barely had spent any time together and already he had something to tell her. This could potentially be a bad sign. Kathryn internally began to brace herself. Did he have five kids? Five wives? What could it be?

"Ever since the day I met you, that day at the conference—do you remember?"

"Of course, I remember. It was…odd, synchronistic, and a little bit, well, magical."

"Yes, yes it was. And ever since that day, I have dreamt of you. Literally, every night you appear in my dreams. At first, I tried to brush it off, tried to ignore the electricity I felt coursing through my body when we met, but the dreams just kept on coming. And then, we were always running into each other—the signs were far too great to ignore."

Scott was talking faster, flushing a bit with each word, yet his confidence remained. She knew he was speaking from his heart. She could actually feel her heart chakra expanding as he spoke. It was if a deeper part of her was responding to his words more than she was able to on a conscious level.

"So, I started writing down the dreams and I realized that they contained a message."

He paused. Kathryn was on the edge of her seat.

"What…what was the message?"

"I don't know if you're ready for this, but after our time at the winery, it was so abundantly clear to me that I just have to say it." He paused again.

Kathryn now felt fearful. And she knew. She knew exactly what he was going to say. Her stomach churned, and her throat dried up. She quickly picked up her water bottle and took a long, slow sip. He waited for her to finish.

"You're The One Kathryn. You're my soul mate. You are the other half of my soul. There's no other way to say it. I've kept it in for so long now and I just can't keep it in anymore. We're meant to be together."

His words picked up speed again and Kathryn felt a rush of energy pulse from her head to her toes. Goosebumps ran up and down her arms and torso. He continued.

"I know, I know, it seems crazy and you have rarely showed any acknowledgement of the energy between us, but I know you feel it. I can see it on your face and I felt it in your kiss at the winery."

And it *was* on her face (among other places), Kathryn was certain of that. But inside, her mind was a whole other story. It was swirling at such a fast pace she could barely keep up with it. How could it be? How. Could. It. Be? She felt the truth of what he was saying and her body was responding at a feverish pace—the goose bumps continued to prickle up and down her body. But, the fact was, he was not Matthew. He was not The One. So, why was he telling her all of this? Why was he dreaming about her? Was the Universe just playing games?

Kathryn's mind reeled from one extreme to the other, as if she hadn't—only moments ago—danced into her body to keep it at bay. Her mind reared its head like an ugly monster, the questions were fast and endless. How would she know the right thing to do?

Kathryn put her hands on her head, rubbed her temples and looked down. She was stunned into silence. They sat there for what seemed like hours, but was, in reality only a few minutes.

Finally, Scott spoke.

"Are you okay? I know this is a lot to take in, but…"

"No."

It escaped her mouth before she could stop it.

"No? No, you're not okay?"

"No, you, me, we we can't be meant for each other. We can't. It's impossible. It doesn't even make sense."

She was finally able to raise her head to face him. He looked at her with such tenderness, with such love, it took her by surprise. It was a look she had never seen before.

"Wait, why don't you think it's possible?" He reached out to hold her hand, and his warmth sent shivers up her spine that radiated throughout her pelvis, stirring feelings of desire. She pulled her hand up to tuck a curl behind her ear.

"It's just that, it's just, oh, it's not important. It just can't be you okay. Not Scott. Not you."

There was no way she could tell him about Samorio, he would definitely think she was crazy. Who took the words of some African psychic as fact anyway? Even she was beginning to doubt her sanity. But still, even though she knew it was insane, a part of her knew there was truth in Samorio's words. How could she explain that to Scott in a way he could understand or hear? He was sitting in front of her expressing his truth and her body was responding in ways that were incomprehensible to her. She had never felt this kind of explosion inside of herself—it seemed to be happening so fast she was unable to

control or discern any aspect of it. While she didn't understand the stirrings that came from deep within, she did know it was unlike anything
she had ever experienced before. And that had to mean something. It
was simply a matter of figuring out what on earth it meant.

"Kathryn. This is one of the most important moments in our
lives. I have been seeking my other half throughout my entire life.
I've been in many relationships, always with the hope that they
might be The One, but slowly over time I would feel it, that same
feeling—the feeling that reminded me that while I was with an important teacher on my path, as all relationships are, I was not with
the woman that was the other half of my soul. When I met you,
Spirit guided me, showing me that you were The One and I was
also shown your fear, which is why I knew it was important to take
things slowly. I wanted to call you the day after we met and tell you
about the dreams and all of it, but that would have sent you running
even further than you already were. So I took my time, but now
Kathryn, now it's time to embrace this magic between us. So, I have
to know, please, tell me why you find us impossible?"

She couldn't believe what she was hearing. He had been on The
Quest, too? He had been having the same experience she was? It really was the most important thing in the world, her soul whispered.
It had been her Quest for a lifetime, but was he really here? What
about Samorio? Her head descended into the spin cycle yet again.

"Thank you so much for sharing this with me. I cannot even
fully express how your words are affecting me. My body seems to
be having its own response—even independent of my mind." She
held out her hands to show him how badly they were shaking. He
grabbed both of them tenderly and kissed each softly. He held them
up to his lips and looked at her.

"Whatever it is Kathryn, whatever the fear is...we can work
through it. We can uncover our path, our purpose together. I will be
here every step of the way. Don't be afraid to tell me whatever it is that

is holding you back. You can share it, and I won't think any differently of you. I mean, how could I? You are me and I am you, really."

With that, he took his right hand and softly stroked her face. He was now sitting so close to her that their legs were touching as they faced one another.

Kathryn took a deep breath. What he was professing was deep, profound love. He was having dreams (she was a bit jealous about this and wished she too had clear dreams guiding her!) leading him to this truth; she at least had to level with him. She leaned down, grabbed her water bottle once more, took a hard, stiff drink, as if hoping the water would purify her and allow her to feel the truth of the moment.

"Okay." She looked him dead in the eyes. "Here's the deal. Right before I met you, I went and saw a psychic who was highly recommended to me by some close friends."

Scott squeezed her hands.

"And well, he told me that my One was named Matthew," she cringed a little as she said this. "And that we would have two daughters and live in Europe, where he would run a sustainable farm."

Kathryn swallowed hard and continued on.

"You see, your name is Scott and you work in marketing and, well, I guess that makes you not The One, which is why I've been resisting this connection with you and instead dating this man named Matthew who, as it turns out, totally does not feel like my One. But he wants to live in Europe and run farms, and his name is Matthew, and it just seemed like that was exactly who I was supposed to be with, but it doesn't feel right with him at all...and with you it feels like—oh—it feels like magic and I keep denying it. And do you know how much energy that takes? It's exhausting. Everywhere I go, there you are and yet I have to keep telling myself that it's not you, you're Scott and Samorio is literally never wrong. I mean, he's from a village in South Africa for crying out loud. He's walked on hot coals and chanted with the gods, and traveled the world, and the gift has been given to him—and I don't understand how he could be wrong, but it feels like it's you and not Matthew, and I just don't know what to do."

Kathryn was speaking so fast, she didn't notice the tears falling down her cheeks or how she was now sitting Indian style facing him on the couch, pleading with him as she explained her story. She also didn't notice that he was smiling, a big, huge smile. He was letting her go on and on, and boy did she. But still he kept smiling, while his eyes also brimmed with tears.

His smiling face and relaxed posture came into her awareness and she stopped.

"Wait—why are you smiling and nearly crying? What's going on?"

As he spoke, tears fell from his face.

"I was born Matthew Scott Lawton."

Kathryn gasped, bringing her hands to her mouth.

"What? Why do you go by Scott?"

He shrugged.

"My parents said I started looking more like a Scott. As a baby they called me Matthew Scott, but pretty soon dropped the Matthew all together and kept the Scott."

"Wow," was all Kathryn could utter. She could not believe what she was hearing.

"And that's not all. Your Samorio really does know his stuff. My great-grandparents started a vineyard in Hungary eons ago, and it's my plan to go back over there when my other half and I have been brought back together…" He squeezed her hands again. "And help transition the practices to be sustainably focused. Most of what the family has been doing is fairly environmentally friendly, but my dream is to take it up a notch and build a solar-powered facility, and manage the farms day-to-day operations while also doing work as a consultant for other sustainable vineyards throughout Europe."

At this point, Kathryn's mouth was wide open. Her thoughts stopped racing and she could hear her heart. "This is THE ONE." Her mind was able to see things clearly. Scott had been The One all along, yet Kathryn could not see it because she was so intent on Samorio's prophecy manifesting in the black and white way he shared it. She expected that her man would be called Matthew—it never occurred to her it could have been his birth name, but not the name he went by as an adult. She had simply assumed that the farm would be a traditional farm with vegetables and animals. It never occurred to her that there were a million different ways Samorio's foretelling could come true.

And despite the Universe's best intentions to show her that it was in fact Scott that she was Questing for, she had completely disregarded all of the signs and instead relied on her own agenda as the way she thought her One was supposed to arrive. She never even bothered to consider the countless possibilities or ways that the Universe could bring Samorio's prophecy to fruition. Kathryn had let her mind do it again—it had chosen an outcome and stuck to it, despite the Universe's signs to the contrary.

There were no words she could utter; for the first time in her life she was completely silenced by her emotions.

So, she did what any girl would do in her position, she leaned in and gave Scott the most delicious kiss she could muster. She started lightly on his lips, and his, hungry for hers, enveloped her, as their tongues danced. Scott pulled her close. Then, he stopped, looked fiercely into her eyes, grabbed her by both arms and said, "Oh, and you should know I'm totally okay with having two little girls."

Chapter 8

"I want to see you.

Know your voice.

Recognize you when you

first come 'round the corner.

Sense your scent when I come

into a room you've just left.

Know the lift of your heel,

the glide of your foot.

Become familiar with the way

you purse your lips

then let them part,

just the slightest bit,

when I lean in to your space

and kiss you.

I want to know the joy

of how you whisper

"more."

–Rumi

Scott led Kathryn by the hand into her bedroom. He motioned for her to sit on the end of her bed, placing his hands gently on her face as he kissed her softly. He gradually pulled away, asking where the candles and matches were located.

"Oh, I can get them…"

He put his finger to her lips and said, "Stay right here and let me do this for us."

Slowly, he lit each candle in Kathryn's bedroom (and there were many throughout the room, put out in the hopes of a man doing exactly this for her. Kathryn couldn't believe her manifestation powers!), while Kathryn sat on her bed watching his every move. His skin glowed in the soft candlelight and she once again was caught off guard by the sexiness of his body, his strong arms, the curve of his jaw, his tight ass…

"Kathryn."

Oops, busted.

"I'm sorry, what did you say?"

He smiled, seeming to know where her mind had wandered off to.

"I said, are you ready?"

Kathryn took a moment to pause. Was she truly ready for this? She knew this was the beginning of something she had never experienced before in her life. She had tried to follow the prophecy she had been given, then doubted, but continued on her Quest ever determined to make Matthew hers, and here she was with the perfect Matthew—the one the Universe had brought to her again and again although she denied him. Now, she was about to surrender. Surrender and give herself fully to the man before her. The man who had not appeared to be The One, but who undoubtedly was her One.

It should have felt a lot more complicated than it did for Kathryn in this moment. There wasn't an inch of her that doubted that consummating this divine union was exactly what she needed to be doing in the moment.

Her smile radiated a brilliant beam of white light from her head to her toes. She had never been more ready for anything in her life. This man was her other half, she could feel it in every cell of her body.

"Matthew Scott, I am more than ready."

"Well then, let's begin."

She had no idea what he meant, but she trusted him implicitly. Kathryn had long dreamed of having sacred, conscious sex with a man, although she wasn't totally sure what that would look like. She had a strong intuition that what she was about to embark on with Scott would be their own version of exactly that.

He came over to her, guiding her gently to the floor. He then placed candles in a circle around them. Kathryn silently applauded her foresight to have purchased all those little tea light holders that were the perfect complement to their divine evening.

Once the candles were in place, he sat in front of her, his legs crossed as well. He slowly took his shirt off, never taking his eyes off of her. Kathryn knew instinctively that she was to do the same, and so she did. They sat there for a moment or two, shirtless, staring into one another's eyes. Carefully, Kathryn reached back and removed her bra. She watched as Scott caught his breath, his pupil's widening as he saw her naked breasts for the first time. She could sense that he wanted to reach out and touch her, but for some reason, he held back.

Next, he took off his socks and stood up to unbuckle and re-move his pants. Kathryn's throat tightened and her heart picked up speed; he was even more gorgeous underneath all of those clothes than he was in them. His abs seemed to glisten in the candlelight and his muscular thighs and legs called to her. She wanted him. She could feel herself getting wet just at the sight of him standing there in his boxer briefs. She too rose to remove her shorts. She took it slow, making sure he watched as she slowly rocked each hip from side to side, pulling her shorts down, ever so gently. She internally whispered a quick "thank you" to her earlier self for having the foresight to choose the lavender lace thong; it hugged her hips elegantly, showing off the feminine outline of her small waist and beautifully rounded hips. Scott took a noticeably strained breath. In fact, she could hear the quickening of his breath and could now see his erection. It gave her great pleasure to turn him on so wildly, especially since they weren't even touching.

They stood face-to-face, nearly naked. Kathryn felt her knees shaking and wondered what would happen next, although at the same time knowing they were co-creating this sexual exploration and she could add whatever next steps she wanted to as well. She decided now was the perfect time to do so. She placed her hands on her hips and nodded at him. He looked at her longingly. She let her panties slide down her legs, never moving more than her hips to allow them to fall down, keeping her eyes focused on Scott's. He tried to hold his gaze to hers, but couldn't. He watched with intensity as her panties slid to the floor. His erection rose even further. Kathryn's wetness was all encompassing now; every part of her body was pulsating, longing for him, longing to have him inside of her. He followed suit, letting his boxer briefs fall to the ground, his sex fully revealed.

Kathryn felt a distinct urge to kneel down and lick and stroke him, but held back. There would be plenty of time for that. She wanted this moment to last forever. Slowly, she kneeled down on the floor, her plush white rug softening her bare knees on the floor, and took a deep breath. She was feeling a little out of control—she was so weak with longing. Scott sat down right in front of her so their knees were touching. Feeling his skin on hers sent ripples of electricity throughout her body. He closed his eyes, placing his hands on hers. Gently, he began feeling her arms, her shoulders, and her neck.

His touch was erotic, sending so much heat to her yoni that Kathryn was sure she would explode. She wanted—no, she needed—to touch him as well. She closed her eyes and began feeling his expansive chest, softly stroking his nipples, then down to his abdomen, feeling all the muscles in his stomach and the hair that softly trailed down to his sex. She lightly touched his erection and felt his entire body tense, straining for her touch. She let her hands explore his pelvis, his thighs, and then back up to his neck and jaw.

As Scott's hands got to know the landscape of Kathryn's body, she felt more and more relaxed. It was like he had touched her a million times before like this, only he hadn't—not in this lifetime anyway. He knew the gentle way to caress her nipples, the soft strokes down her abdomen and to her heat. He lingered there and Kathryn's breath became jagged. Her yoni was pulsating so strongly she wanted to arch herself right into his hand, but she held steady. He glided his fingers along her labia, teasing her clit, and circling her yoni. She was dripping wet. He gripped her thighs, feeling her legs and settling in on her feet. Their touching had reached a fever pitch. Kathryn opened her eyes, Scott was staring at her.

Kathryn smiled gently. It felt so incredible to feel this man—how had she been able to deny him for so long? It was impossible for her to understand. But now, looking into his soulful blue eyes, she reminded herself: everything was happening perfectly and exactly as it was meant to. He leaned in and kissed her softly, nibbling on her lips, and then the intensity picked up—she could feel his longing and she too could barely restrain herself. They arched into one another, their bodies clinging to one another on her bedroom floor. Slowly, they rose to their feet in unison, never parting lips, bringing their bodies fully flesh to flesh. Scott pulled Kathryn into him, gripping her ass, wanting and needing her desperately. Her hands cupped his face; she was trying desperately to take him in all at once—and it was too much and too perfect at the same time.

She felt his erection against her, and no doubt he must have felt her heat radiating from her pelvis outward. They were as close as they could be skin-to-skin, knowing their exploration would soon lead to completion—for this first encounter, anyway.

Suddenly, Scott pulled away, looking at her.

"I want to remember this moment for the rest of my life. I want it to stay burned into my brain, so that no matter what happens in our lives together, I can always access this memory. You are the most gorgeous, loving, sexy woman I have ever had the divine pleasure of having in my life. Thank you for this gift."

Kathryn felt tears welling up in her eyes, while she still struggled to understand the various emotions flooding throughout her body and soul. On one level, she was more turned on than she had ever been with a partner. She wanted to devour this man, she wanted him inside of her, filling her up, she wanted to ride him until she screamed and shuddered with orgasm. And at the same time, her heart was so full, so filled with love and adoration and…gratitude. The Universe hadn't lied, it hadn't conspired against her as she had thought in some of her lowest moments. He had been here all along. She merely had to let him in.

"Scott, this night will never end. In our hearts, spirits, and bodies it will always live. Thank you for giving me this gift. I am overcome with so many emotions. The strongest of which…" She stepped in closer, just an inch away from him…"is my desire to be consumed by you in every way."

He took a deep breath, smiled sexily, and swooped her up in his arms. It took her by such surprise she let out a small yelp followed by laughter. Then, ever so gently, he placed her on the bed. He leaned down, kissed her, and said, "Don't move, I'll be right back."

And he wasn't lying. In a matter of seconds he was back with a condom in hand, and ready to complete what they had begun so many months before. Kathryn couldn't help but smile at his preparedness.

As if reading her thoughts, he said, "We're not ready for those two girls just yet, are we?"

She giggled. "Absolutely not."

⌒

Kathryn woke up first as the morning light streamed in, feeling Scott's body pressed against hers, holding her as they lay together. She sighed, a contented, loving sigh. This was right where she belonged. Their love-making had been intense, soulful, and expansive. She never knew it could feel quite like it had. He was with her the entire time, never escaping into his own world with his eyes closed, but rather watching her, talking to her as his body moved rhythmically in and out of her. He was gentle, yes, and even more so was very careful with her. His touch, his gaze, his movements—he wasn't just sexing her, he was loving her.

Their eyes stayed locked on one another and when Kathryn could no longer keep her orgasm at bay, he asked her to keep her eyes open as much as she could. She had never done this before. Usually she closed her eyes when she came, allowing herself to be sucked into her own world where the pleasure unfolded, never able to fully share the experience of divine oneness with her partner. But, she knew this was different. Scott was the other half of her soul and co-creation in their union was paramount.

When she climaxed, she thought (and hoped) it would never end. She forced her eyes open, forced them to lock onto his as the waves of pleasure flowed through her entire body. He whispered to her, gently telling her how much he loved her, how he had searched for her endlessly, and now they were together at last. When finally the ocean wave of her orgasm calmed, Scott let her know he could no longer hold it in and that he too would come, wanting to fully share what his unfolding was like with her. Kathryn was overpowered by the look in his eyes combined with the energy she felt whooshing and flowing between them. She felt the lifetimes they had spent together, she felt his desire and his love, and for him, she whispered words of adoration and affection.

They lay there afterwards, smiling, holding hands, taking turns looking over at one another and saying repeatedly, "Thank you." That's how they had fallen asleep, and now as she lay awake, Kathryn was once again overcome by the joy radiating throughout her body. Something was different, she was different. The contentment she felt lying wrapped in Scott's arms went deeper than she had ever experienced. It was so deep inside of her that she didn't know where she stopped and he began. Her intuition whispered truth to her— this man and their union would forever change Kathryn and her life.

The Quest was over.

Chapter 9

"The soil needs the seed, and the seed needs the soil. One only has meaning with the other. The same thing happens with human beings. When male knowledge comes together with female transformation, then the great magical union takes place, which is called Wisdom."
–Paulo Coelho

The day after Scott and Kathryn spent their first night together, Matthew sent Kathryn an e-mail. It was as though energetically Matthew could feel that something had changed between he and Kathryn. Some part of him seemed to know that Kathryn no longer needed to hear from him, and was no longer interested in capturing his love in any way. As surprised as Kathryn was to hear from him, she also knew it was no coincidence. It was time to lay the craziness that she had been engaged in with him for the past few months to rest. She had to meet with Matthew to tell him the absolute truth of what had transpired since their ill-fated first date.

And after spending two days fully in the presence of Scott's love, she felt like a completely different woman. Kathryn felt as though she stood taller, her skin glowed, and the Universe was continually working in her favor (in fact, she had just scored an amazing writing gig with one of Portland's famed lifestyle magazines about sustainability and community!). She felt more grounded in her life, as if she was living on purpose for the first time. Suddenly, she was sure of everything. She knew what she wanted and when she wanted it, whether it was groceries, a new writing gig, what outfit to wear, the color of flowers to buy—any and all of it. The confusion was gone, her mind stopped its racing games, and there was only calm combined with total knowing and gratitude.

It was this high vibration that she took with her as she walked down NW Portland's 23rd Avenue to meet Matthew at one of her favorite cafes, Vivace. As she walked into Vivace, Kathryn was greeted by the smell of coffee brewing and the coziness of the space (once an old Victorian home and now a cutesy café with tables and chairs tucked into every nook and corner of what used to be someone's living and dining rooms). She ordered a peppermint tea and waited for Matthew to arrive, taking in the relaxing atmosphere, barely aware that a huge smile was plastered on her face. Matthew, however, noticed immediately.

"Kathryn, you look stunning—in fact, you're glowing!" he said as he quickly gave her a hug and a peck on the cheek.

She put both hands on her cheeks, "Am I?"

Of course she was being coy. She knew full well that coming together with her soul mate was the reason why she felt nothing but bliss. She might as well have had a sign around her neck that said, "I met The One."

"First off, Kathryn, before you say a word, I just want to apologize for the way I acted a couple of months ago before you went to Brazil. I don't know what happened to me. It was totally unacceptable and I want you to know how sorry I am. I tried to reach out to you, but we kept missing each other and then I got absolutely swamped at work. Clients seemed to suddenly fall apart and needed my immediate help—I'm sure you know the drill. I hope you can forgive me. I'm so, so sorry."

While it was nice to hear his apology, it seemed like lifetimes ago that she had left Matthew's apartment, crying and uncertain. Those days were a faint, distant memory at best. She could see the whole scenario so much more clearly than she did during it. And this was how life worked. Once the storm passed, one could see the true reason for its occurrence, along with the lessons to be learned.

Kathryn placed her hand on Matthew's, and he jumped back a bit, looking startled. He clearly wasn't used to being touched in such a way—as a friend or not.

"Matthew, at the time I was very upset and angry. I thought, well, I thought you were The One."

This revelation made him sit back even further, scooting his chair away from the table and raising not one, but both eyebrows.

"I know, it's ridiculous, but hear me out." Kathryn said, putting her hand out as if try to reel him back in. It looked as though he might leave at that very moment.

"Before we connected at the networking thing that Jess hosted, I saw a psychic and he said I was going to meet and marry a man named Matthew who would manage sustainable farms in Europe. I was so hypersensitive to hearing the name Matthew that once I realized it was your full name, I was like white on rice to you. As I'm sure you noticed," Kathryn rolled her eyes and smirked, showing Matthew she realized, now, how silly she had behaved.

"Then, on our first real date when you told me about your fantasy to manage farms in Europe, I nearly fell off my chair."

Matthew stared at her in disbelief, leaning into the table, although still keeping the chair in its distanced position. "What are the odds that I would say I wanted to do the exact thing the psychic told you?"

"I know! That's what I thought. So, I was just sure it had to be you, but as you know, our connection was never quite…on. It seemed like we were crossing wires a lot and not on the same page at all. It was incredibly frustrating for me, I simply couldn't understand. Meanwhile, I was getting all of these signs and synchronicities that were putting this name Matthew in front of me—so I kept coming back to you thinking that there was some way that you'd notice, too. Every part of me was like no, not The One, but the Matthew prophecy kept reeling me back in again and again."

"And yet, we continued to miss the mark with one another. I mean, we couldn't even connect via phone or in person for what's been over a month now. I couldn't figure that out for the life of me. It was like we were being blocked from each other," Matthew reflected.

"Exactly. Finally, I gave up—at least internally—and I let myself open up to this awesome man, Scott, who I kept randomly..." Kathryn gave air quotes for effect, and Matthew smiled. "...running into for the past few months. And, you'll never believe this..."

Matthew had brought his chair back to its rightful position and was now leaning into the table in such a way that he was practically on the edge of his seat.

"His first name is Matthew and his middle name is Scott, but his parents have always called him Scott."

"No way! Again, what are the odds of that?"

"I know, right?! AND, it gets better. His grandparents live in Hungary and he plans to take over their winery, manage it *and* make it totally sustainable."

Matthew's mouth dropped open. He looked as dumbfounded as Kathryn had when Scott shared all of this with her.

"Holy shit."

"Yep, that about sums it up."

She placed her hand on Matthew's again, and this time he let her.

"So, I wanted to meet you today to apologize for how crazy I have been acting throughout our time together. I wasn't myself; I was a hot mess, actually. Everything in my body was telling me something was wrong—you weren't The One, but my mind was intent that you had to be because you matched the prediction the psychic gave me so accurately."

"God, Kathryn that makes so much sense. I wasn't myself either. I found myself getting so triggered by every little thing. I could feel your intensity, but didn't know what it was about. I'm definitely at a stage in my life where I want to play the field and sleep with lots of women."

Matthew turned a little pink at having said this out loud. "I mean, you know, I want to have fun and date. I've even been exploring polyamory as a possibility—you know Portland has a really big poly community."

His ears turned bright red as he revealed this. "And while I really dug you, I could tell you wanted more than what I was able to or wanting to offer. I kept thinking that I would tell you all of this, but I couldn't find a way to behave normal around you. I would just close up emotionally whenever you were around. So, I'm the one who's sorry, really, truly sorry for all the miscommunication and confusion."

They smiled at one another. It was amazing how openly communicating could shift things around immediately. Kathryn saw with absolute certainty that Matthew had never been the guy for her, nor would he ever be. A man who wanted to sleep around with the possibility of having more than one girlfriend? PDX trend or not, it wasn't for her. She knew she was here to do the work with her other half. She could not believe that she had let her stubborn mind force her to keep reaching out to Matthew and continue going on dates, even when it felt so…well, wrong. And here he was speaking his truth. He wanted to get laid (clearly) and have fun, not be with his soul mate. No wonder they were triggering one another and acting completely unlike themselves.

"You know Matthew, I am grateful for our experience together. It showed me how much more I need to honor when something doesn't feel right—regardless of what anyone else is telling me, including amazing, always-right psychics from Africa."

Matthew chuckled.

"Yeah, especially those guys. Actually Kathryn, I'm so happy we've had this conversation and that we've been able to share what's truly been happening for each of us. Thank you for your openness. It's allowed me to open up more fully too and finally claim what I want. I need to share this with any woman who is interested in dating me or vice versa. So, thank you, because your lesson is also my lesson. It's so clear that your integrity and your actions must always be first for yourself. You have to listen to your body, to your intuition, to your guidance—whatever you want to call it—when it's screaming at you. We see people every day who haven't done this, right? I mean practically 90 percent of the population is living from their mind, not their soul."

Kathryn nodded, knowing that this was one of the main reasons why she was on The Quest. Practically everyone she knew was in a relationship or a job because they were scared not to be, more than because it was in their highest good. They ignored their bodies' many signals—the illness, the random events that made life that much tougher, the nagging in their gut saying something wasn't right—all because they were far too terrified to face their truth. Their spouse or career or whatever it was, was not a perfect fit for them at all. But instead of facing this truth and expanding the way their soul was urging them to, they argued that nothing was perfect and life was hard—all in an effort to deny what they knew was true deep inside.

It was the biggest lie ever told.

Life was meant to be fun and easy and connected. It was meant to feel good. And when it didn't feel good, it was a sign that an individual needed to bring his/her life back into alignment with his/her soul.

Matthew continued. "We see them everywhere. People who have made the choice to settle. Who haven't listened to the longing in their hearts that said, 'That One now!' or 'Go for it!' It somehow became safer for them to settle. And what an empty existence that is. I know you could never do that, and neither could I. I'm excited to step onto my path more fully now because of this conversation, and I'm so thrilled that you opened yourself to Scott, and discovered that he is your One."

Kathryn couldn't believe the way everything was unfolding. Without the supposition that Matthew was "The One" she was able to see him clearly for the first time. He was a great guy—just not *her* great guy. He cared about living from his heart and following his soul's guidance, and he even understood the importance of doing so. But, what Kathryn was really admiring about him was that he was tuned in enough to his guidance that he would not sacrifice or settle for anything less. Kathryn had been trying to push herself and him into something that fit because she wanted it so badly. Because she did this, she wasn't able to see anything clearly.

Matthew, on the other hand, was showing her that honoring one's truth (whether it's getting laid or finding The One) was the only way to live. Kathryn would have been exactly like one of the many people she witnessed living not to fail, living with the belief that having a shitty job or relationship was better than not having it at all. Living a lie. This conversation with Matthew was yet another validation of her path, her truth, and her connection with Scott. Her eyes once again brimmed with tears of gratitude.

Matthew noticed this, looking at her with more kindness than she had ever experienced from him previously. They had healed something important here—for both of them. As a tear streamed down her left cheek, Matthew reached out and gently wiped it away.

"I hope those are tears of joy and not tears of sadness for having wasted several weeks on me," Matthew winked.

Kathryn laughed. "They are absolutely tears of joy—I feel so, so grateful. You know, for so long I thought the Universe was pissed at me and was stubbornly refusing to deliver what I asked for just because. Ridiculous, right?"

"It's a little bit ridiculous, yes."

Laughing harder now, Kathryn went on, "And come to find out, it was working in my favor the *entire* time. It's so bizarre. Now, Scott and I are delving into this next phase and it's magic. Seriously, magic. The psychic also said we would have two daughters, and –"

"I thought you didn't want children."

"That's the thing, I never have. I can't even imagine being a mother. It doesn't seem like something I would be good at, I'm too afraid I would mess them up, you know?"

"Oh, I hear you—that's why I have no desire to propagate the species…"

"Well, all your girlfriends might want to have a word with you on that."

Matthew laughed. "You may be right. But seriously, Kathryn, how will you resolve that? Does Scott want kids?"

It was so odd, from the time Kathryn was at least 10-years-old, she was certain she would not be a mother. She simply had no desire. When women talked about yearning to have children (she even had a friend who said her womb ached with longing to be a mother), Kathryn was completely dumbfounded. It was as if that part of her was dead. She felt nothing. She thought babies were cute and sweet, but she always felt afraid that she would drop them or hurt the child in some way. And so, she stayed away from other people's babies. She had helped care for her sister as a little girl, but that was as far as her experience went with little ones.

When Samorio gave her the prophecy, she felt like getting herself into kid-mode was the least of her worries. She just wanted to meet The One already. And now, she had. This meant she was going to have to face her negative aversion to having children at some point. Several years prior, another intuitive told Kathryn that she had two souls circling her, souls who wanted to come into the world through her. She just laughed and told the intuitive to tell them they would have to wait—until another lifetime. It wasn't that she didn't like children—she did, she just never imagined having her own. Ever since she was a child, she felt like she would skip the whole kid thing. As the oldest, she had seen what her mom went through raising Audrey. It never appealed to her.

"Yes, Scott does want kids. And it is something I should look at healing. I've always said I could skip the kid thing, but if it's part of my path to give birth and have children," Kathryn shuddered as she said those words. "Then, I better figure out what the block is."

"Well, I have every confidence that you will. But, in case you're interested in getting a little help with that process, there is an amazing healer I know who does a lot of work with past lives. She does body and energy work to help clear blocks that remain from previous incarnations. If you're interested, I can send you her info. This could possibly be a past life block."

Kathryn immediately shook her head yes. She didn't have anyone in her healer sphere that worked with past lives. "Matthew, thank you so, so, so much. I so appreciate it."

Matthew was already at work on his phone sending her the information. He looked up, grinned, and said, "Thank you Kathryn. You are truly one in a million. You should have that e-mail when you arrive home!"

With that, Matthew stood up from the table, stretched out his arms, grabbed Kathryn, and gave her a big hug.

She could feel his warmth, something she hadn't felt before, and was stunned by the rush of love and gratitude that swept into her soul for him. He was such a necessary part of her journey. She had to force, had to "try" to make him work, so she could finally give up, open up, and let her true One, Scott, in. And what healing had occurred for both of them by sharing their truth! Matthew could now embrace his yearnings and join the PDX polyamory community, while Kathryn could focus on love—her love with Scott and unraveling their mystery together, including what her true blocks were about having children. It seemed so silly now that she had battled in her mind about whether or not a man who ogled women in front of her could be The One. She had completely forgotten that the only place she ever needed to go was inside her heart. Brazil had reminded her of that important lesson. Her heart was the only place she would ever find her answers.

Matthew had been the guiding light all along—he had led her to trust her heart and fully open to love. As he walked away and Kathryn set out to stroll the streets of Portland's Alphabet District, she gratefully looked up at the heavens and smiled.

The Universe had known what it was doing all along.

Chapter 10

"There are only two ways to live your life. One is as though nothing is a miracle, the other is as though everything is a miracle." –Albert Einstein

The days and nights that followed flowed by effortlessly, and very quickly. Scott and Kathryn were inseparable. When they had to be apart for work or other outside commitments (like Kathryn's weekly ecstatic dance classes), they used text and phone to stay connected.

"I love you Kathryn. Every minute of every day."

To the average person this might seem nauseating. For Kathryn, it was a dream come true. She had always imagined that true love would be full of romantic gestures, open communication, conscious love-making, and adoration. And with Scott, it was.

Often, they stayed up long into the night, on her couch, legs entangled, sipping red wine and talking. They discussed spiritual principles of reincarnation, the possibility that they were in fact soul mates; they discussed finances, how they enjoyed spending their money, their dreams of where they wanted to live and what they hoped for in their lives. Neither of them had ever felt more aligned with their partner. They shared a gratitude list every night with one another, listing the top five things they were grateful for.

Scott always listed Kathryn as his first item. This, of course, made Kathryn swoon.

In fact, every aspect of their relationship made her swoon. She couldn't believe how her life had transformed. She was quite literally living her fairytale. However, the conversation with Matthew about having children had continued to tug at her since their meeting. She had told Scott about it and mentioned that she wanted to do some healing work on her blocks of bringing children into the world. Scott had looked at her from his position across from her on the couch, one hand leaning up against his ear and said, "There's no hurry love—do what you need to do and I'll be here. And just remember, we don't have to do anything we don't want to do—psychic reading or not."

That kind of support was incredibly comforting, because Kathryn feared that what she might discover in exploring her blocks to having children was that she absolutely should *not* be a mother. She was afraid that someone would confirm her fear—she would be terrible at it. The more she tried to toss the fear aside, the more it reared its ugly head. It was even seeping into her dreams. Kathryn kept having dreams that she was responsible for a baby and would then go about her day, completely forgetting about the child. In one dream, she left the baby in the car all day and forgot to feed it. Her mother was there to scold her. In another dream, she was responsible for watching several toddlers and left them up in an attic to play and again forgot to feed them. When she finally remembered, she ran up the stairs and apologized to the kids. One of them in particular looked at her and smiled, saying, "Don't worry, it's okay."

Kathryn knew this all meant something. It was coming up for healing and it was something she needed to look at now. And so, she took Matthew's reference and made an appointment with a healer named Sally.

The morning she was set to see Sally, Kathryn woke up with a headache. As she began to get ready for the day, Scott too sensed that she wasn't feeling well. Only, he seemed to feel that it was something far deeper than Kathryn imagined.

"Are you feeling concerned about your healing session today love?"

"Um, I don't think so. Why do you ask?"

"Well, you've got that headache and as you said, you never get headaches *and* you've been sort of pacing around this morning, dropping things, cursing," He smiled. "Which as you know, I find very sexy." He leaned in and gave her a juicy kiss, letting it linger for moment. "But still, it's not like you. You feel a bit off to me and I'm wondering if it's because your soul knows there are some big shifts coming."

"Wow, honey. I hadn't even thought of it like that and I'm supposedly the woo-woo one in this relationship." She snapped a towel in his direction as they both navigated around one another in the bathroom. "I was taking it all pretty much at face value, but if I feel into it—which is the one thing I haven't been doing this morning—I definitely feel a weird tension. There's some resistance for sure. Almost like I don't want to go."

"Do you want to go?"

"Yes, because I know I need to address my fear around having children. But on a deeper level, I'm really freaked out and feel the urge to avoid the whole thing all together. Any words of wisdom for me?"

Scott leaned in to kiss her one more time as he said, "Just be open to whatever unfolds, baby."

⌒

When Kathryn arrived at Sally's, she was pleasantly surprised to find a cozy home space with a crackling fire, decadent red and orange throws, beautiful water colors, and a tall blonde woman with huge green eyes and a kind smile.

"Hi, I'm Sally. You must be Matthew's friend Kathryn."

"I am, so nice to meet you. And thank you for seeing me."

"Oh, of course. I've been working with Matthew for years, so when he refers someone to me, I know it's going to be someone who is also doing deep, spiritual work."

"That's so sweet. I hope you can help me release some of the blocks that I seem to have."

"Well, that's my specialty. However, as I mentioned on the phone, I don't want you to tell me too much about what blocks you're looking to release—I want your spirit to tell us what's happening. Is that okay?"

"Actually, that sounds perfect, thank you."

"And I see you followed my clothing instructions perfectly. Just dress down to your sports bra and workout pants and lay face down on the table. I'll be in in a few minutes and we'll get started."

Kathryn was left standing in the room, a string of chills buzzing up and down her spine. Something was amiss. She shuddered and pangs of fear spread through her belly. Her head continued to ache.

Even so, she did as instructed and laid down on the table. She was surprised to find herself easily drifting off into a meditative state while the lovely ambient music played in the background. It seemed like it was taking Sally a long time to come back, but Kathryn wasn't bothered. The music was relaxing and she was enjoying the bliss of getting into an alpha state.

As she was drifting peacefully off, she was aware that Sally was once again back in the room. Without saying too much, Sally began working on her—some of it felt like massage, coupled with some work in her energetic field, above her body. And as Sally continued, the work intensified. Kathryn felt like she might cry. Sally must have sensed this, because she said, "Are you doing alright over there?"

"It feels really nice, but I feel an intensity picking up and for some reason my eyes are welling up with tears."

"That's actually perfect. I'm picking up on some current life stuff with your dad right now. So, just let those tears flow."

The topic of her dad was not one Kathryn liked to discuss. He had left her, her mom, and her sister when she was 10, and had only occasionally bounced in and out of her life. She felt abandoned on a deep level by him—something she had spent many years working through in therapy and with a form of energy medicine that worked with one's Soul alignment called BodyTalk. Seeing her mom and sister in such pain when he left made Kathryn vow she would never put herself or anyone else in a position to be hurt like that. It occurred to her that some of the reasons why she was afraid to have children could be tied to that. She didn't want a man to leave them high and dry. The vision of her mom and Audrey curled up on her bedroom floor crying the day her dad left would forever haunt her. Kathryn, the oldest, felt she had to be strong, and when she saw what was happening, she chased her father out the door screaming at him for making her mother cry.

The tears fell in huge drops onto the floor (luckily they fell through the massage table's face cradle) as this scene replayed in Kathryn's mind. She connected to her 10-year-old self. The self that said no man would ever do that to her or her children. Ever. What better way to protect herself than by never really getting close enough to a man to have a child?

But now, now that she had met Scott, she had to let it go.

Some time passed as Sally continued to work on her, and the tears kept flowing. Then Sally stopped, and so did the tears.

"Yep, I think we got that released. There was a lot of pain there, you poor thing. How are you doing?"

"I cried a lot and saw the scene with my dad that impacted me the most. Crying it out helped. I don't know that I ever cried before for that part of myself."

"Well, you did a beautiful job releasing it. Let's now have you turn over. There's some past life stuff that wants to come up."

By now, Kathryn was feeling excited to know more. If she could have an incredible release from whatever Sally did to her back and legs relating to her current life, she couldn't imagine what might be in store when Sally worked on her past life blocks.

Just like before, Kathryn couldn't tell if anything was really happening, so she let her mind drift, sure that something would get her attention when it was time for it to. Suddenly, something did catch her. Sally had one hand on Kathryn's pelvis and the other under her low back, on her sacrum. Chills began running up and down Kathryn's body, but she had no idea why. Her mind frantically raced to make sense of what was happening.

Then, as if something or someone else was taking over her body, Kathryn began to move. She sat halfway up, feeling the distinct urge to push as tears began streaming down her face. The chills now rolled over her in waves, and Sally was acting as a guide.

"Breathe Kathryn!" Sally yelled. "You have to let this happen, you have to let it move through you."

Kathryn's tears turned into sobs, her body shaking, knowing that something terrible was about to happen. Her mind continued to race to understand what was happening, but it was lost, unable to place this memory or this event into any present day context.

Quickly, Sally moved her hand from Kathryn's low back to her shoulder and started giving Kathryn instructions.

"Move your legs, and then push them apart when I count to three, okay?"

"What's happening?" Kathryn cried.

"Just let this happen, okay? Don't fight it."

"I don't want it to happen," Kathryn cried. "I don't want my baby to die."

"We have to do this Kathryn." Sally stared into her eyes firmly. "It's time to release this." With that Sally began to count, "One, two, three—push Kathryn, push!"

With that, Kathryn pushed her legs apart and screamed. This time she was sitting all the way up, her hands gripping her inner thighs as she leaned forward sobbing. Sally stood next to her, softly rubbing her upper back, letting Kathryn cry.

Finally, she was able to stop. She couldn't believe how exhausted she felt. She lay back down, looked up at Sally, and whispered, "What just happened?"

"Well, I don't want to color what was happening for you with my interpretation. What do you think happened?"

"I think…I think I relived a birth I had. Before. But…" Kathryn's eyes began to well up with tears once again. "The baby didn't make it. He…He died." She was sobbing again.

Sally soothed her.

"Yes, that's what I was feeling, too. And there were so many guides in the room with you during that. In fact, I can feel the presence of the baby now."

"It's a boy, isn't it?"

"Yes. Something happened and the sense I got was that the cord was wrapped around his neck, so…"

"With every push, I was strangling him."

"Well Kathryn, you had to push—otherwise you would have died."

"So, in another life I killed my baby?"

"In another life, your baby died during childbirth. You know, childbirth is very dangerous, babies and mothers used to die all of the time. It was not your fault."

"Thank you for that, but during whatever just happened, I felt it—I felt him dying and me trying to get him out, but knowing it was going to be bad if I did. It was so overwhelming."

"And what are you feeling now Kathryn?"

Kathryn's mind had completely given up trying to make sense of any of this, although in the back recesses of her mind it screamed,

"This is crazy!" And even though it *was* crazy, certifiable even, she could not discredit what she felt, how the chills and sobs came, how she knew it was a birth she was reliving, how she knew it was a baby boy that was meant to come through her. She knew it—without explanation of any kind. She scanned her heart and soul. What was it saying now? All she could hear, very softly was this: "I'm so sorry. I'm so, so, so sorry. I'm so sorry."

Kathryn began to cry again.

"What is it?" Sally asked quietly.

"All I can hear are the words, 'I'm sorry,' again and again."

"The imprint of the woman you were in that lifetime is still living within you, and she does not need to be sorry anymore my dear Kathryn. That is why the boy is here with us now. That's why this is happening now, today. The imprint of that past life has created extreme guilt over this event and it is keeping the boy from being able to move on in his life progression, and it's keeping you from fulfilling your path in this lifetime. Haven't you ever wondered why you never wanted to have children? Didn't you know it came from another time, another trauma?"

The thought of being stuck or unable to complete her path from something that happened lifetimes ago was aggravating to Kathryn. How could it happen? Was this truly why the thought of giving birth both terrified and disgusted her? Was it this memory lodged in her psyche that kept her from creating a life that involved children? It never occurred to Kathryn that a past life could have such a powerful impact on her current reality. She had no idea how to navigate something like this.

"What can I do?"

"Go deep into the recesses of your soul and talk to this former life that still has a hold on you. Let her know it's okay, the boy is okay and you're okay. It wasn't her fault. She has to release him and she has to release you. It will allow everyone involved to be at peace."

"But she is me? This is so confusing, I don't understand."

Kathryn's mind was starting to get involved again.

"This isn't something your mind can comprehend logically Kathryn. You have to feel your way through it. You've just relived a very traumatic experience for your soul in a past lifetime. Your personality, the part of you that is Kathryn in this lifetime, can relieve your soul of this pain. That's why this has come up now; it's ready to be healed."

Despite her mind's ability to charge in, Kathryn could still hear "I'm sorry" over and over again within the area of her heart. She focused in on it, went deep within, and could feel now her soul's warmth. It felt like a warm, cozy blanket—one she had worn a million times. In fact, she probably had. She felt so much love—it was all-encompassing and brought tears to her eyes. Not sorrowful tears, but rich, loving, joyful tears. She was connecting with who she really was. And this time she heard a message.

Kathryn took a deep breath. Her mind uttered, "You might be losing it Kathryn." She ignored it, flicking the thought away like an annoying gnat. Instead, she focused on sending her soul—and the imprint of a former life—love and compassion, soothing it, letting her know it was okay, there was nothing wrong and nothing to be sorry for. She spent a few minutes doing this by saying over and over, "It's time to let this go, everyone is okay, you did nothing wrong."

It took some time, but after a while, she felt something inside of her smile. And then she had the knowing that the past life imprint that was grieving received her message. Tears of joy slid down Kathryn's cheeks. Never before had she connected with any of her previous lives in such a tangible way. She had healers over the years mention various past lives, but she never paid much attention. She was once told she had a life as an African woman with a small child. As she journeyed across the desert to get her child to a safe village, she died and so did her child.

Kathryn shared this with Sally.

"It seems as though I've had other lives where my children have died. I never, ever made the link that this could be connected to why I have no desire to have children in this life. But, could it be?"

"Oh, absolutely. That guilt was strong. I don't know if you realize it Kathryn, but you were screaming and sobbing so loudly, it was disconcerting. I could feel your pain through your cries. You released something very big today. Something that has been holding you back in other areas of your life."

It was true. Kathryn had broken up with men if they were intent on having children, and even though she clung to Samorio's prophecy, she rolled her eyes at the thought of having two daughters. For her, it wasn't a possibility. She figured she would worry about that after she had attracted her man. And now that Scott was in her life, the babies would be something she would have to think more about. She figured that Scott would understand if she didn't want to have children, but now some part of her felt that having children was part of what she was meant to do in this lifetime to fully complete her life purpose.

The session was over and Kathryn felt absolutely spent. She was set to meet with a potential editing client for a new Paleo cookbook that afternoon, but knew she would have to cancel. All she felt like doing was sleeping. Sally encouraged her to honor this feeling and to be very gentle with her body as it had been through a major trauma. Kathryn noticed her lower back ached and her knees were weak. It boggled her mind, nothing had truly happened—at least not in the three-dimensional world—just like with her psychic surgery in Brazil. Yet, it was as though losing her baby during childbirth *had* happened, all over again.

On the drive home, Kathryn wondered what she would tell Scott. She didn't want to bring up the issue of children too soon. Hadn't she burdened him with enough of her psychic weirdness?

But, in her heart, she knew she could tell it all to him, and that he could handle it. Or at least that's what her heart hoped the outcome would be.

She was curious how her perspective might change toward having children now that she had the session with Sally. Would she feel differently? Even now, immediately after the experience, the thought of having a child didn't seem so awful and traumatic. It didn't feel like something she wanted to run out and do, but she felt something inside of her open up, just a crack. She wondered about that woman she was many, many moons ago. The pain and agony she felt wanting to have a child and then losing it during childbirth. How she must have suffered—suffered so much she made sure there was a part of her soul that would never allow that kind of pain or agony again. She would replace it with caution and fear, and shut down the natural part of her that yearned to bring new life into the world.

Kathryn had spent a portion of her life thus far focused on her Quest, but simply pushed away any thoughts of having children or being parental. What would she do now that The Quest was over? After the session with Sally, Kathryn knew that children would somehow be part of this next phase in her life. And what did that even mean? She had no context for a life with children in it. Despite her confusion, she felt like she needed to share this healing with Scott to get his perspective on how she could best process all that had occurred that day.

She sent him a quick text.

Exhausted from today's healing session—big stuff addressed. Going 2 sleep for a while and will share it with u when I can make more sense of it. Miss u!

Scott texted her back immediately after.

No worries babe—take your time and bring it up when it feels right. B gentle with yourself and I'll see u this evening. I'll bring some wine and dark chocolate. I love u.

Kathryn had slept all day long, popping in and out of consciousness only to awaken to unclear dreams that vanished as soon as she
opened her eyes. When Scott arrived, she had managed to move
herself onto the couch, but still had her pajamas on—charcoal gray
lounge pants, a white camisole and a long heather gray sweater.
Immediately, he gave her a big hug and kiss, holding her tightly.
Then, he turned and headed into the kitchen. Kathryn noticed that
he seemed a bit preoccupied. Something was definitely on his mind.
She wanted to talk to him about the healing session, but didn't
know the best way to open up the conversation; she wasn't exactly
convinced that she wasn't completely insane about the whole thing.

Normally, she would review something like this with Jess, but she
wasn't ready to share it with her just yet. In fact, Jess had sent her
a text right after the appointment asking how it went. All Kathryn
could get out was:

*It rivaled my experience in Brazil and now I have 2 go home and sleep. Talk
with u about it when I feel I can express it without sounding nuts.*

Of course Jess understood, although she did ask for a hint.
Kathryn had texted back. "Re: baby." Jess wrote back with an
"OMG!" that made Kathryn smile. She had known about Kathryn's
aversion to having babies, so she was sure Jess would be intrigued
to learn more. But first, Kathryn needed to talk to Scott about it. If
she could get a word in edgewise, that was.

As he poured Kathryn a glass of Smoking Loon Merlot, he began talking about Hungary. He started talking a lot about how much
he loved Hungary and the winery—all of which Kathryn knew. She
was excited by the possibility of spending their later years in life
running a sustainable winery. As her mind wandered off and on
about her healing session, it focused in as Scott said, "And it had
been my plan to return to the family vineyard by next year to begin
taking over the management of it."

This caught Kathryn off-guard. Early next year? She loved living in Portland, and while Samorio's prediction had always included living abroad, she imagined that would be much further in the future—like 10 or more years. She didn't want to raise their children (wow, she really was thinking about this kid thing in a different way!) without her family around. If she was truly going to do this baby thing, she would need her mother around. Her mom was practically a baby guru and had already helped many of her friends bring their little ones into the world. She loved it. Kathryn's mom was the birth coach, the infant support, not to mention the best babysitter a daughter could ask for. Having a baby—if she was actually going to have one (or god forbid, two!)—was going to mean having close family support.

She had to find a way to explain this to Scott so he would understand.

"Honey, it's so incredible how passionate you are about the winery, but I honestly cannot imagine going over there so soon. There is so much more we need to do here. I want to be here with Audrey and my friends and our community. And if we do want to bring some little ones into the world, I can't do that without my mom's support. In fact, there's something I have to tell you about…"

"Babe, I love how much you love your family and Portland, but this is my, our, destiny."

He cut her off, in fact, she was pretty sure he didn't even hear the last part of what she said. She wasn't even able to tell him about how profound her healing session was. Unfortunately, he didn't seem to notice her staring at him with her mouth wide open.

"Think of how amazing it will be to live on a vineyard, in a whole other world. We can create the family we want. People have babies every day without their families around—we can too. Besides, a lot of my relatives are still there—and sure they're distant, but we'll form bonds with them. And I'll make sure that early on we fly you home at least once every six months for a few weeks at a time.

You're so good at making friends and attracting positive people into your life, I know that we'll find a great, supportive community as well. We'll be able to do this, and it's going to be amazing."

This didn't sit well with Kathryn. Didn't he understand that she would be having the baby? She would be the one reliving this past life trauma? Didn't he understand that it was the woman who got saddled with the majority of the burden of having children? She couldn't just leave everything behind to do it all on her own in some foreign country with people she and Scott barely knew. There was so much here in Portland for her—she just couldn't imagine leaving it all behind. For anyone.

She attempted to smile lovingly at him, but was boiling inside. Would her "One" really expect her to abandon everything she loved just for him? Could he be so clueless about what truly went in to bringing a child into the world? What happened to co-creation and making decisions as a couple?

When she shared this with Scott, his ego got engaged as well. Soon they were both defiant in their positions, holding their ground. Kathryn insisted that the move happen far later in life after they had built a solid foundation together and she was ready to write books full-time. She argued that she wanted their children to be American citizens. In truth, Kathryn didn't know where any of her lame arguments came from. If someone had asked her yesterday if she wanted children, she would have said "maybe" at best. But once her ego got triggered, once she thought that Scott was trying to run her life, all bets were off.

She was now somehow patriotic, when she had never cared one way or the other. In fact, she had often fantasized about how amazing it would be to live in another country, experiencing a totally different culture. But, that wasn't the point. She was in defensive, adversarial mode now. Scott strongly disagreed with her; seeing the opportunity to move to Hungary in the next year as an opportunity to build their own life while partaking in work that was meaningful and made a difference for his family and the local Hungarian community.

It was their first, real fight. Kathryn was near tears when she said, "I think you should stay the night at your place."

This was the first time she had said this or anything like it. Normally, neither of them could bear to leave one another at night, and they vacillated between his place and hers depending on what the other had going on the following day. It seemed as though Scott was just as entrenched in his position as well.

"I couldn't agree with you more," he said. He briskly pressed a kiss on her lips, held her at arm's length and said, "I love you." And then he was gone.

Kathryn had only been able to whisper her feelings in return. "I love you, too."

Once the door closed behind him, tears streamed, in large drops, down her face. How could this be happening? Why would the Universe let her soul mate drag her away from everything she loved and that was important to her? How could he be so selfish? Briefly her consciousness whispered to her—she was doing it again—pretending to be the victim of the Universe, pretending that she didn't understand the laws and how they worked. Her mind was in control.

With horror, the thought occurred to her: maybe Scott wasn't her One. Maybe it had all been a mistake and they had placed their fantasy into one another's stories. Perhaps The One was still out there, looking for her—the man who loved her more than anything and wanted to live life just as she did.

The next day came and went, and the day after, too. Kathryn did not reach out to Scott, nor did he reach out to her. They were at a total standstill, and it didn't appear that anyone was going to budge. Kathryn found herself in a full-fledged negative loop. She, unfortunately, remembered this pattern from before. She had been here before. The feelings were the same. At some point in every relationship she had ever been in, she found something about the person that she was convinced was insanely in opposition to her. It could be the friendship he had with a woman she was sure was in love with him (she wasn't, and two months later he became engaged to a totally different woman and was now happily married), it could be his desire for even more alone time, or his relationship with his mom (he talked to her every day and soon the sound of the phone ringing grated on Kathryn like nails on chalkboard), or his difference in spiritual and political beliefs (one man would never be a fit for her no matter how wonderful he was because she couldn't let go of the fact that he was a registered Republican—although he claimed he voted more along the lines of Independent).

The fact was, no matter the man, no matter where she was in life, Kathryn would find something that didn't feel right and would then focus all of her attention on that one thing until it was so big it was the only thing she could see when she looked at him. The negative thought cycle would perpetuate itself, as it always did, and before she knew it, she was saying, "I can't do this anymore."

She knew herself well enough to know that this was the beginning stages of this exact pattern with Scott. Scott, her soul mate. She couldn't even connect to the part of her that imagined their life with children. She knew this was a sign that she was internally shutting down. She needed to do something quick to stop the cycle before all of her ingrained defense mechanisms took over.

She pondered all of this as she trudged along on a long walk. Just then, her phone rang. It was Scott. At first, she wasn't going to answer, she wasn't in a positive enough place. But, something deep inside tugged at her.

"Oh, hey," she said as she picked up the phone, trying to sound as nonchalant as possible, even though they hadn't spoken in two days.

"Hey, Kat, I miss you."

His voice cracked.

She just wasn't there yet.

"I'm glad you called," it was as close to positive as she could get.

"I really think we need to talk face-to-face, I've been doing some serious thinking about all of this. I love you and I don't want to have anything come between us. Especially not something like this."

She sighed, feeling her heart begin to open back up to him. Just a crack anyway.

"I don't want to fight either babe—ever. I don't know how to get over this. It feels like such a big hurdle."

"I know it does, and I could feel you detaching from me. And that's the last thing I want to have happen. Have you been meditating and getting in touch with your guidance?"

The truth was, she hadn't. She had been stewing about Scott, focusing on how he could potentially not be The One, and lamenting the fact that she may have to start up The Quest yet again. It was odd, because she noticed that some part of her felt a bit excited about this. The option of new possibilities was seductive. So seductive, Kathryn hadn't been able to pass it up before.

"Well, not, um, not really. I've been sort of trapped in being angry and feeling justified in that anger. I didn't get a chance to tell you about the intense healing session I had the day of our argument. It had a lot to do with our future and releasing my fears around having children," she admitted.

"I know, honey. I thought about that later. I was so eager and, to be honest, nervous to talk to you about Hungary, it didn't even occur to me to ask you about what happened for you during that session. I'm sorry it was so tough. I can imagine our conversation triggered even more fears about the future, especially if you were to be in a foreign country where you knew no one."

"It absolutely did, but even if the kid thing wasn't an issue, leaving my home and everything I've worked for is not appealing to me. At all. But, um, I probably should be taking that to meditation, journaling, and prayer."

Kathryn could feel the slightest hints of old anger boiling up inside of her again. It was tough to admit that she hadn't been doing her work, only marinating in her negativity about the situation.

"One of the things I love about you Kathryn is that no matter what is happening, your self-awareness is so deep, you can call yourself on your own shit."

She giggled, relaxing a bit into their conversation. Doing that made her feel like she wanted to see him right away. He went on.

"So, can you do me a favor?"

"Depends on what it is..."

"Okay, I would love to see you sooner rather than later, but I would like for you to take tonight to really go inside yourself to see what this is about for you. So, that way when we see each other tomorrow night, you're really clear about what this triggered within you. Then, we can have an honest conversation about our relationship and let our stubbornness go. What do you say?"

"Tomorrow night?" It seemed sort of far away. She wanted to talk with him more about the situation now and share what had happened during her healing session.

"Yes, I'm going to take you out on a special date tomorrow night. We'll have an intimate environment to connect in for this conversation, I promise."

"Well, I love a surprise, so you're on. I do need to go inside myself and see what this is about for me. Have you done the same?"

"I have and I'm sorry I acted so strongly. I think we can come up with a way to work through this, but we both need to be open to the possibilities."

"Okay, I hear what you're saying. And you're right—there has to be a way. I'll start now; I'm on a walk so it's a perfect time to quit stewing and start tuning in."

"That's my girl. I love you Kathryn. Forever and always."

"I know you do babe. And I love you so much. Thank you for being the bigger person and calling me first. Sometimes I'm far too stubborn." She felt a smile return to her face.

When she hung up, she felt like she had been able to raise her vibration to a positive level just by talking with him. The walk seemed less like a task she had to complete and more like something she wanted to do to connect with her inner guidance. She had opened up to it during Brazil and she was so grateful that Scott reminded her to go there for this situation. She had such a hard time accessing her intuition when she felt rooted in her particular position. It was during these times that access to her soul was somehow cut off from her, somehow shut down by the negativity. The walk would help her quiet down inside, as the conversation with Scott had. Going home and meditating would help her get in much deeper as well. She breathed a sigh of relief. She was ready to do her work and stop blaming Scott and the Universe.

After she returned home, Kathryn began preparing for her meditation ritual. She lit candles around the house, turned her Pandora on to "New Age Ambient" (one of her favorite relaxing stations), drew a bath filled with Epsom and sea salts, and lit some lavender incense to clear the air from the argument and the harsh feelings that had been created by both of them.

Stepping into the bath felt good to Kathryn's body. Her mind was still chattering, now bubbling with possibilities that Scott could really be The One, turning over all the options for how Hungary could be part of her story. She still didn't want to move right away, but was hopeful that together they could come up with a workable solution. Children didn't feel awful or a must—simply neutral. There was a lot of ping-ponging and chatter happening within her mind.

Once she sank down into the water—with it covering every bit of her body from her chin down—she felt the chatter soften. She focused in on the lovely sounds of the music and closed her eyes. She saw herself and Scott, dressed in white on the beach somewhere warm. She saw his smile and aqua blue eyes. She let her fingers trace the outline of her body, imagining his touch. For the first time in two days, she felt herself fully relax.

Kathryn lay like that for what seemed like hours, until she felt ready to meditate. Her skin was squishy and soft from the water and she let herself take her time, applying her body lotion, choosing her favorite white chemise for the rest of the evening. While she continued to pamper her body, she suddenly felt the urge to skip the meditation and instead watch a movie or pick up a book— something other than go into her soul. She had noticed previously during moments like these in life, when she really needed to go within, some part of her would fight it, would resist receiving the wisdom that lay within her. And that was her sign to journal before she started the meditation. There was something more within her that needed to come out. Healing was possible, but only if Kathryn willingly engaged it and let it in.

Finally, she was ready. She sat on her comfy couch, her hair piled high atop her head and pulled out her journal. She wrote the date, the time, and her location—"Home on couch"—before she began. She liked to imagine that after she was a famous author, she would look back on these journals to see how far she had come. Or perhaps she'd be like her idol Paulo Coelho, and someone would want to write her story. Anything was possible, and Kathryn always enjoyed thinking big. She closed her eyes and let her hand move, letting the words fly. The first thing she felt was fear, fear that Scott was The One. She was surprised to find that there was more fear about him being The One and her having to do her work within the confines of an intimate partnership than fear that he was not The One.

What if Scott is The One and I fail?

What if I ruin our relationship somehow?

What if I don't know how to be truly happy?

Kathryn couldn't bear it. Some part of her, some part of her that loved her and wanted to protect her, felt it was safer if she detached. That way she couldn't find out that her worst fear was true—that she was totally unlovable.

Sadness continued to bubble up and out onto the page. Pain she thought she had long let go of came up to be revisited—being left, first by her father and then the boyfriends that followed, feeling judged by her family and small community growing up for bad choices around the type of men she dated (in her twenties Kathryn had a penchant for rebel bad boys with tattoos and rough, addictive attitudes). There was still a lot of fear left from these experiences and while Kathryn was surprised to find it there, some part of her had always known that it still existed. She let her hand go and it kept on writing. She knew her hand would stop when she was done.

About an hour and 15 pages later, Kathryn was finished. There was so much written down, she couldn't believe she had written it all. Some of it probably didn't make any sense, while other portions contained clarity. It didn't matter, she didn't need to re-read it now. What mattered was that it was out of her psyche and on the page. Next, she lit a new batch of incense and grabbed her Doreen Virtue Goddess cards. Now, she would begin meditating, and then she would ask the cards for validation and information about what she needed to do next.

It didn't feel right to set a timer; Kathryn wanted to sit in meditation for as long as she needed. She didn't want constraints now. She needed the freedom to do what was best for her soul. While consciously she wasn't sure what that was, she wanted to be free to allow it to unfold the way that would bring her the most healing. So she sat, the ambient music playing softly in the background, her mind drifting back and forth from chatter to peace, on and on like the waves of an ocean. She felt herself slowly drifting in and out of consciousness until her eyes opened—letting her know she was finished. She often meditated this way, going until her eyes opened and her soul seemed to let her know, "You're done now."

Taking a deep breath, she looked around her cozy apartment, smiling. Everything was going to be okay. She was being supported and it was all happening the way it was meant to—whatever that meant, she wasn't sure, but it did make her feel better. Kathryn grabbed her Goddess cards and began to shuffle them, asking silently, "What do I need to know about Scott and I? "Is he 'The One?' Show me what I need to know about Scott." She shuffled the deck until she felt the pull to stop.

She took another deep breath and flipped over the card on top. Her heart leapt. "Guinevere—The Goddess of True Love" stared back at her. The card said, *The romantic stirrings in your heart have propelled the universe to deliver great love to you.* The cards, as she had experienced, were never wrong.

Kathryn had her answer. The card was the final validation of what she had been feeling (and yet continually denying for so long!). With that, she knew what she would say to Scott tomorrow evening. She knew not just because the cards told her he was her great love, but because in her journaling and meditating, a theme had appeared. An addiction had presented itself. Kathryn had been able to see herself more clearly than ever before.

In fact, she had learned a lot about herself during this night of soaking, tuning in, and meditating. And most importantly, she had learned something that had never before occurred to her.

She was addicted to The Quest.

Chapter 11

⌒ᗡ

*"If you are brave enough to leave behind everything familiar and comforting
(which can be anything from your house to your bitter old resentments) and
set out on a truth-seeking journey (either externally or internally),
and if you are truly willing to regard everything that happens to you on
that journey as a clue, and if you accept everyone you meet along the way
as a teacher, and if you are prepared—most of all—to face (and forgive)
some very difficult realities about yourself…then the truth will not be
withheld from you." –Elizabeth Gilbert*

It had been with Kathryn, her entire life. It was what she was good
at. She could date with the best of them—she loved going out on
dates, meeting new people, and thoroughly enjoyed the dance of
trying to figure out if the man before her was "The One." And it
was easy for her. It simply took her one date to "know" if the guy
was "the guy" and she was fastidious about honoring her original
judgments. She loved reading books about finding "The One"—
trying new techniques to call in this perfect man that would be her
other half. She had practically made it her second career. That made
it even easier to abandon the notion of having babies. Who had time
for that when there were so many more exciting things to focus on?
Why unearth her past life experiences of pain and trauma around
motherhood when she could instead try out the newest restaurant
with a man that had (in her imagination) all the *potential* of being The
One?

162

God, it was so freakin' obvious. Kathryn's addiction to The Quest ran deep.

And in those moments, when Kathryn was exhausted from trying to find him and sitting opposite of yet another man who seemed more enamored with her light and her Quest than his own, she rewarded herself with dark chocolate and red wine, along with many "Where is he?" sessions with girlfriends. While she was successful in her career and felt deeply fulfilled with her personal relationships, her struggle always centered on finding her man. She should have seen this coming. The Law of Attraction is the most powerful law in the Universe.

If you focus all of your energies on finding The One, sooner or later—despite carefully crafted unconscious sabotage techniques—he's going to come in. Kathryn had always assumed that they would live happily ever after and the rest would be bliss. And the truth was: the Law of Attraction had worked for her—very, very well. She always met men that would be nice boyfriends. But always, something would feel "off" or not right. Maybe this was because he wasn't Scott, but a deeper part of her knew it was also because her addiction to The Quest had made it impossible for her to see any real long-term potential with anyone. She was bound to place the same judgments on Scott if she wasn't careful. She had already begun to do so.

Kathryn shook her head laughing. She had been so naïve. Nothing in life worked with 100 percent perfection—what would be the fun of that? It was her job to be conscious. Besides, Kathryn logically "knew" that relationships were where the greatest growth occurred—they were the biggest teachers. Why would she expect The One to be completely absent of any challenges or struggle? That was the whole purpose of being with the other half of your soul. She had just heard famous relationship expert John Gray say that, on average, every couple has up to nine points of incompatibility. Nine! Conflict and seeming incompatibility was absolutely natural. But to Kathryn, one sign of non-alignment meant she was back on The Quest.

It was pretty mind-blowing to feel the part of her that missed the familiarity of The Quest. It was a part of her that would stop at almost nothing to get back to that comfortable place. Kathryn realized, quite shamefully she had to admit, that she was not comfortable with being in a happy, peaceful relationship. She didn't even know what that looked like beyond six months, a year tops. By seven, eight months into any relationship, she had methodically uncovered what was "wrong" and stayed fixated on it until she was so miserable that she had to leave the relationship just to feel relief.

But, Scott was different and Kathryn could not let the relationship with him go the way it had with all of the ones before him. He was her "One"—she was sure of it. And any doubts about that came from the place within her that didn't feel like she deserved to be happy and loved. She had to break that cycle now.

Scott was right to suggest that Kathryn do her work before they met up. Had they met sooner, she would have been liable to put the entire situation all on him. Unraveling it in this way made her face a big truth. She may have superficially "let go" of her life Quest, but it had by no means let go of her. She needed to go deep within herself to identify what was truly happening inside of her.

Only now, she had to figure out what to do with the new knowledge that she was addicted to The Quest…

~

Scott picked her up freshly shaven and smelling of her favorite cologne, Eternity by Calvin Klein. He kissed her gently, whispering, "You look beautiful."

Kathryn blushed, looking down briefly at her emerald green cocktail dress and then peering up at him. She had wanted to have an impact on him—several days without talking or seeing each other was quite difficult. She wanted him to swoon when he saw her. And he did. "Thank you, you smell delicious," she said, leaning in to kiss him again.

The car ride had been pleasant, but uneventful. Kathryn wasn't sure what she was feeling. She was happy to be near him, just being in his presence soothed her, but that was all she could make out. She didn't want to push things and try to force a conversation. Besides, she had taken a workshop by Alison Armstrong that said to never, ever try to discuss anything of importance with a man when he was driving. Men were one directional. They needed to focus on getting you wherever they were going.

So, Kathryn let it be. Scott was playing one of her favorite CDs, Band of Horses, and she let the soothing sounds carry her away. He was taking her to Andina in the Pearl, known for its excellent Peruvian food and Malbec wine (well, at least that's what Kathryn knew about it). Once they arrived, the energy began to shift. When Scott opened the car door and she stepped out, she felt it. The heat, the dizzying electricity between them. It was palpable. She took a breath and smiled.

Scott, always able to read her mind, said, "You feel that too, huh?" and then winked.

God, he was so delicious, she wanted to take him right there in the middle of the sidewalk. But Portland's elite Pearlites were not apt to appreciate such a raw display of...er...affection. Never mind that right now anyway, they had some serious negotiations to embark on, and if Kathryn wanted it to go the way she hoped, she would have to take her focus off his hot presence and focus on her heart. It was going to be tough, but she had to do it. To ease the sexual tension building within her, Kathryn had to remind herself that she would have him later, as in right after their dinner. Perhaps even in the car—depending on what the Universe offered them.

He must have arranged things beforehand, because just as he

promised, they were seated in the back of the restaurant, tucked in near a window, away from most of the people. It was a beautiful and intimate atmosphere to connect in, neutral yet flowing with excitement and decadent smells. Kathryn smiled to herself; Scott always seemed to know what they needed—even before she did.

Breaking them out of their trance, the waiter approached as they sat there smiling at one another. They must have looked so silly Kathryn thought.

"Good evening, can I start you both off with something to drink?"

Kathryn looked up at the waiter only to find herself staring into the eyes of one of the most gorgeous men she had ever seen. It actually caught her off guard, and she found herself stuttering over her order. Scott came to the rescue, saying, "Babe, don't you prefer Malbec?"

"Oh yes, yes, I would like the 09 BenMarco Malbec please," she stared up at him again, smiling as seductively as she knew how, her eyes instinctively opening and closing widely. Her heart nudged her to focus. But something else was pulling her.

The waiter—whether or not he understood energy—responded in kind, "Of course Madame. And I must say, you look very beautiful this evening."

"Why, thank you," she felt herself blushing like a schoolgirl.

If Scott noticed this, he didn't say anything. Rather, he began talking about the menu and the possibility of choosing a few dishes to share together. Kathryn, on the other hand, couldn't concentrate. Something was off, she needed time to re-center. She interrupted Scott as he read from the menu.

"…grass-fed lamb grilled to order…"

"Scott!"

He looked up, startled, and only then did he see something amiss on her face.

"Are you okay?"

"I'm feeling a bit off. Will you go ahead and pick out whatever you think sounds good and I'm going to make a brief trip to the ladies room to re-ground myself. Is that okay?"

He grabbed her hand. "Of course. Do you need anything? Did something happen?"

"No, I just need to take a few minutes for myself. And the grass-fed lamb sounds excellent."

Kathryn squeezed his hand.

Scott seemed worried, but steadied himself. "I'm right here if you need anything. Take your phone with you, if you need to go we can. Just let me know." His brow crinkled a bit, confirming that he was definitely worried. She had only seen that look one other time on his face and that was when she first told him that they were "impossible."

Kathryn walked away from the table and sighed. She couldn't believe she was doing this. She didn't need to worry him right now, but she also couldn't continue their intimate dinner while making googly eyes at the waiter (who did she think she was anyway? Matthew?). This was far too serious for any of that.

On her way in, she saw the waiter looking over at her. She smiled tightly and hurried on to the bathroom. She needed to get clear about what she was doing or rather what her addiction to The Quest was doing. If she wasn't careful, she was apt to be carried right out of there and into the arms of some waiter who she would then embark on her usual pattern with. If he made it that far—Kathryn surmised he had a one-to-three date maximum. The Quest could keep right on going if Kathryn wanted it to. Did she?

In the bathroom, she began to take deep belly breaths and started tapping Cortices—an energetic tapping technique that balanced the left and right hemispheres of the brain and allowed her to re-connect to her higher consciousness. Then, she placed her hand on her heart, willing herself to connect with the deeper part of herself. The waiter and she had a physical attraction and that was perfectly normal, but she didn't want to live like this anymore—seeking, searching, noticing the attractions and wondering what it was about. She wanted…wait…what did she want? Where was it? She searched inside her heart:

"Where are you," she asked?

Two more deep breaths brought her back to Scott. She saw his face looking at her, felt the way he touched her, and remembered all of the divinely glorious ways they had been brought together. She was surprised what a tight hold The Quest still had on her. It was as though in identifying it last night, it was coming back even more aggressively. But she had to let it go. It was time.

It was a hot waiter for god's sake. She couldn't let something like that throw her off.

But, how did one let go of an addiction like The Quest? She intuitively knew she had to surrender to the Universe, surrender to the knowing that there was something greater in this world for her. And one of those greater things was Scott. She knew it; she felt it through her whole being. The attraction with the waiter was just that—an attraction—aggravated by the fact that she was about to go all in with Scott, holding nothing back and diving into the life they would create together. A life she had never imagined for herself, but one she intuitively knew was right for her.

It was terrifying, yes. It was completely unlike anything she had ever done before. She didn't know how to do it. She didn't know if she would be good at it. She didn't know if she would even like it every day (in fact, she was quite certain there would be days when she didn't like it at all). But even so, if she was truly committed to this path, if she truly wanted to live from her soul, to do the work she was sent in this lifetime to do, she would have to let go of this addiction.

Finally, the knowing returned. She moved her hand down to her solar plexus and felt into her soul, and it whispered, "You are on the right track. Go back to him."

And so, Kathryn adjusted her strapless cocktail dress, smoothed her crazy curls, and headed back out to Scott. She didn't even lift her eyes to meet the waiter's and walked up to Scott's chair. She leaned down, put her hand behind his head and kissed him. The minute their lips locked the knowing whispered to her again, "This one."

Scott put his hands around her waist and placed her on his lap. There they were, in Andina, in front of the window for all of the Pearl to see as they made out at their table.

Kathryn pulled away, placing her hand on Scott's face and said, "I'm yours. Whatever it is, wherever we go, as long as you're by my side, I'm going to be okay. I know it."

His eyes glistened.

"Yes. There is such great love here and I cannot imagine my life without you. Let's work together to find the best way to make this work."

"Deal."

Kathryn leaned in for one more kiss before pulling away to sit in her own chair, which now felt miles away from him. She could still feel the heat of his hands, his skin, and his lips on her, even from across the table. She wasn't about to get thrown off track again. The best way to beat a pattern that has been dogging you for years? Consciously choose a new route. Kathryn's determination was back. She would fight for this. It was the life she was meant to live.

By the time the food arrived, they were two glasses into their Malbec and settling plans on where they would live and what they would do in their new place. They devised a plan that made them both comfortable: they would wait two years before moving to Hungary, giving them both time to attract the money they wanted for their new life and to fully enjoy living in Portland. Kathryn would quit freelance writing/editing once they moved and focus solely on her career as a novelist. Scott would fly her back to Portland every three months to see her family, and would fly at least one member of her family over every year for a few weeks. They would be in Hungary for at least three years and from there would decide if it was something they wanted to continue doing. They could stay at the vineyard or move on to manage other vineyards as the opportunities presented themselves.

Ultimately, their intention was to make the vineyard so successful, and for Kathryn's books to be such bestsellers, that they could live half the year in Portland (July through October, when the weather was absolutely perfect and no one could argue in favor of anything except that it truly *was* the best place on earth to live) and the rest of the year in Hungary or wherever else they might like to be. Truthfully, though, it didn't matter. Kathryn and Scott were both committed to living from their souls, following their guidance, and the signs from the Universe. They would make the choices that felt the best to them, as the opportunities arose. What mattered most was that they continued to work together and choose one another, again and again.

Holding hands in the candlelight, the rest of the restaurant buzzing around them—people laughing, going here and there—Kathryn felt the same peace she had during that first night with Scott. She had returned to her original intention—being with her One, the man she loved more than anything in the whole world. The Quest might try to rear its silly head every now and then, but Kathryn knew with untold certainty that she was exactly where she was meant to be.

"And what about those two little girls Samorio promised you?" Scott teased.

"Hmm…well, we're probably going to need to practice," Kathryn said as she slowly drew her foot up Scott's leg and gently nudged his inner thigh with her heel. "A lot of practice. And from there, we'll see what the Universe gives us."

Scott leaned across the small table and kissed Kathryn. He smiled at her and said, "Shall we get started now, or wait until we finish the lamb?"

⟿

A few months later, Scott and Kathryn moved in to a brick townhome on Portland's west side, and only then did she decide to return to see Samorio. This time it wouldn't be for a fortune, but to express her gratitude.

Samorio smiled as he saw Kathryn walk up to his porch in southeast Portland. He was sitting outside enjoying the fresh air.

"You are happy, my dear Kathryn. You must have found your Matthew."

Kathryn's face widened into a grin, "Yes, yes I did Samorio. But he wasn't at all who I thought he would be."

"They never are, my dear, they never are. Please sit down with me," Samorio motioned to the other rocking chair beside him. "So, tell me, how was he different than you imagined?"

"I got caught up in the name and tried to make someone else fit, completely ignoring the signs from the Universe that were telling me that the Matthew that kept turning up everywhere I went, was in fact, the Matthew I was meant to be with…Even though his name didn't totally match up at first."

Samorio chuckled.

"It is our greatest challenge as humans to trust the Universe to take us where we have asked to go, surrendering our control, and releasing our preconceived notions about what anything in our life should look like."

Kathryn sighed. Here it was all along, the truth. She had been fighting herself and the Universe for far too long. She was more than ready to surrender to it.

"So, I didn't even need to come to you and ask you who it would be. I could have just followed the signs and my intuition the whole way through and found my Matthew Scott."

Samorio turned so he was directly facing her, his face suddenly serious.

"That's exactly right Kathryn. You never need me or anyone else to tell you anything. Everything you need is within you. But, we forget this and are desperate for reassurance. And that's why I think the gods have given me this gift. To bring a little relief to the human desire to know more about their lives. Although, as you discovered, having that knowledge—if we don't trust and surrender—can make things even harder."

He was saying his words slowly as if to make sure Kathryn was taking in every single one of them. He was giving her a message for the future, she was sure of it.

Samorio reached out and touched her arm and looked at her firmly.

"You have everything you need Kathryn," he said softly. "You just have to believe it."

Kathryn's eyes welled up with tears as she threw her arms around Samorio.

"Thank you so much Samorio. You have been a great gift to me."

He laughed and said, "Except when I wasn't."

They both laughed at the humor in this. When it comes to handing out predictions, a psychic is either god or the devil. Kathryn knew this all too well. Her days of needing to ask for truth outside of herself were over now. She stood to leave. She was on her way to have a celebratory dinner with Scott, Audrey, Jess, and Hillary and Paul at her favorite sushi spot, Uchu.

"I won't be seeing you around will I Kathryn?"

She smiled.

"Nope. I'm off to surrender to the Universe, in the fullest sense."

With that, she took off down the street, beaming. Her world was completely different than it was six months ago when she asked Samorio to foretell her future. The celebration could truly begin, because Kathryn was living without The Quest. Leaving it behind meant she could do whatever love led her to.

And so, she would go to Hungary and have Scott's babies and anything else love asked of her...

Go Deep! Discussion Questions for The Quest: A Tale of Desire & Magic

✳ Kathryn receives a detailed prophecy telling her who her One is and that they will have two daughters together. What has been your experience with intuitives and psychics? Have the predictions been true? What did you learn from having those experiences?

✳ Kathryn has a synchronistic encounter with a stranger while seeing Abraham-Hicks for the first time. When have you also met someone in this way, perhaps running into them a few times in a row? What ended up occurring from this connection and what message did that person have for you?

✳ When Kathryn and Matthew have their first date, Kathryn is at first unsure about their connection but as time goes on the alignment with Samorio's prophecy becomes evident and she surrenders to their connection. When have you felt unsure of a person or situation only to find that it later is a better fit for you than you initially thought? In what ways would you like to open yourself up to new people and opportunities in the future?

✳ Kathryn and Matthew's second date brings up a huge trigger and insecurity for Kathryn. What sort of situations or environments serve as triggers for you? How have you worked with them in the past and how could you address them differently in the future?

✳ Scott and Kathryn have a strong connection at Kirtan that really throws Kathryn for a loop. She is struggling profoundly with "decoding" the messages from the Universe and is trying to integrate Samorio's prophecy into every occurrence. When have you found yourself caught up in decoding messages as opposed to listening to your heart? How have you found ways to slow down and reconnect to your truth no matter what is happening around you?

✳ Kathryn's experience at John of God was intense and brought up a lot of fear for her. What is it in life that brings up fear for you? Can you see how fear is always a conditioned response if true danger is not present? In what ways can you work with your intuition so that you can decipher when your response is intuitive or based on your previous conditioning?

✳ On the wine tasting tour Kathryn and Scott come together in a powerful way. What's the most powerful connection you have felt with another? How did it impact your life?

✳ Kathryn and Scott experience conscious sex with one another—something Kathryn had only hoped would happen for her at some point. What is most important to you when it comes to being sexually intimate with your partner (either existing or soon-to-be)? How can you bring more conscious intention and connection into your sexual experiences now—either with yourself or another?

✳ Once Kathryn had been able to let go of the story that Matthew was "The One"—she could see him more clearly and appreciate him for who he really was. Is there someone in your life that you are not allowing yourself to see clearly? How might you shift the energy of that dynamic so that you can more clearly see the person and create an even better connection?

✳ Kathryn experiences an important discovery when she realizes she is addicted to a negative thought cycle that causes her to leave relationships and continue questing as opposed to doing the real work of being in a deep, intimate partnership. What areas in your life do you allow yourself to engage in negative thought cycles that keep you stuck? What are some rituals or action steps you can take to free yourself from these patterns and raise your vibration?

✳ Surrender is something Kathryn comes to understand is absolutely necessary to live her life fully in love and abundance. What are some areas in your life you feel ready to surrender to? And what does it look like for you to fully surrender?

About the Author

 HEATHER STRANG is an author, Certified BodyTalk Practitioner and Shambhala Multi-dimensional Reiki Healer. Her books include *The Quest: A Tale of Desire & Magic* (currently being optioned as a feature-length film), *Following Bliss,* and *Anatomy of the Heart: Love Poems.* Heather became interested in holistic healthcare after using energy medicine to heal herself—first via John of God and then using BodyTalk. Heather now blends the power of BodyTalk, intuitive wisdom, positive psychology, the Law of Attraction, and John of God healing energy to facilitate a host of courses and soul alignment events. These events support individuals in claiming the power they have deep within their bodies to create an abundant and sexy life.

Heather holds a BS in Liberal Studies with an emphasis in English and Women's Studies from Portland State University, and graduated summa cum laude. When she is not engaged in some form of work-play, you will find her meditating in her pajamas, dancing down the aisles of the grocery story, and/or exploring the possibilities of the Universe through books and travel. Heather currently resides in Portland, Oregon, but is ready to go wherever her Higher Self takes her. Learn more about Heather at: www.HeatherStrang.com